XXX

The Underground

Playgrounds

by

Ms. Pantha Jones

Take Over Publishing LLC

Gary, Indiana 46404

Paperback Version

ISBN-13 978-0-9824338-4-3
ISBN-10 0-9824338-4-0

Cover artist: LRB

Beware

PROLOGUE

"I can't believe this shit!" Doll screamed, as she paced back and forth in Donovan's 9,000 square foot home. She had been this way for days. How many days? She was not sure. However, what she was sure of was that DMX stayed in the expensive stereo system. She had plummeted into darkness and X was the only one that seemed to know that pain.

X pills, weed, and a bottle of Van Gogh, continuously invaded her body, and not in that order; consuming food only when she had the munchies. Did she go insane? She had to be insane to still be in this house with that repulsive smell. She had been waiting days for him after his phone call. The 9mm never left her hand. She was contemplating killing herself after she killed him. She didn't see any way out of this shit. She didn't think anything else could mend her destroyed heart, but his blood.

She could just imagine what the headlines would say about their beloved football star and his crazy fiancé. Their hometown of Gary, Indiana loved their Native son and the Indianapolis Colts named him MVP, even though he was just a rookie. Therefore, she knew if something was to happen to their precious Don, it would be all over the news and Internet.

Her father said she was crazy like her mother. Repeatedly, she could hear his voice as if he were standing right there. "You're never going to be shit. I should just take your ass to an insane asylum and be done with you! Get me some money off of you! Something wasn't right in your mommy's head and ain't shit right in yours!"

"NO! NO!" she screamed, as she threw bottles at the voice. Something wasn't right in yours, you crazy son of a bitch! You were constantly beating her ass and fucking women right in your own bed! You drove my mother crazy and I'll be damned if I'll be like her!" she yelled at her father.

His voice was still taunting her, laughing at her, as he used to when she was younger. "You see what you have done and you say you aren't crazy. HA! I told you about that bitch. When you were growing up, I told you to stop being friends with her. HA! Now she fucked your man and guess what? You gave her permission, just like your dumb ass mother! Her father's laughter echoed around the house. You should kill yourself like your mother did.

"NO! YOU EVIL MOTHER FUCKER!" She kept throwing objects at the darkness, finally silencing the voice.

HER MOTHER

Her memories were always intact, too vividly sometimes. It was plenty of things she would have liked to forget. Snug in her princess comforter, surrounded in the princess's World of Walt Disney, she waited. She knew at any moment that her father was going to make the little girl come sleep in her room with her. It only happened once in awhile and at first, she didn't mind; she thought it was a game of pretend. How wonderful for an only child to have someone to play pretend with her, but as she grew older, she knew it was something wrong with that situation.

It was something wrong with her household. She might've had everything a little girl could have possible want, and then some, but her household was functional psychotic.

"Now go lay with your Baby Doll, so you girls can a have a slumber party." Her father said.

Rolling her eyes in the back of her head, Doll hated hearing her father talk like that, because usually he belittled and smacked her, but now since he wanted her out of the way until the morning, he treated her like he did Doll. She had no idea what went on out there. Her father had rules and one of them was to not leave your bedroom at night without permission, unless it's an emergency.

10

The little girl happily jumped in bed with Doll, taking utmost of Doll's full size bed, because of her height. The little girl kissed Doll on the cheek, which made Doll smile inside, for no matter who she was today, a kiss from her made her feel loved.

A child like voice came from behind Doll, "Let's watch a movie, Baby Doll," she giggled, as she turned on Doll's flat screen T.V.

"Momma, let's just go to sleep," Doll said seriously.

"Momma? Silly, I told you I'm not your momma, Baby Doll. Can you keep a secret?" The little girl asked, getting close to Doll's ear. "Your momma disappears when your daddy is a bad man. They always send me out here to protect your mother because your father is always nice to me." Her mother smiled at her, as if they were school friends, and she told her she had a secret crush.

As this version of her mother flicked through the channels, having idle girl chat, she lay there confused. How many different people were in her mother and which one was her real mother? Was it this little

11

girl? Was it the docile weak woman that let her father hit her and talk down to her? Was it the normal mother figure that was around when her father was at work? Was it the woman she often caught a glimpse of any time her mother had a blunt object in her hand, glaring and sneering at her father? Which one was her real mother and how would she know she's the real one?

"Unh Unh. I'm nothing like my mother," she tried to convince herself as she paced back and forth crying. She kept looking in the bedroom, hoping that what occurred had not occurred, a couple of nights ago. She had been waiting for him to come home since yesterday. She had to do something with her pent up anger, until he got there. It felt good throwing those buckets of fish guts onto his 10,000-dollar bed, in all of his dressers, in his walk-in closet, and let's not forget his vintage gym shoe collection. The cars were next and maybe she'll do a Left-Eye.

"He deserves it! He fucking deserves it," She screamed out!   She heard Don's car drive up, peeked out the window, and saw her best friend get out of the passenger seat. She couldn't even describe the feeling that she was feeling. She ran quickly to the basement's wine cellar and waited for them to come in. Her mind flashed to when it all begin...

The Proposal

Being swept off to Miami on a whim was nothing new to Doll. That was just the way Don was... Spontaneous! Lounging on the yacht all day, cruising, and just enjoying each other's company, Doll wasn't aware of the plans he had for them.

"Doll Baby, why don't you go downstairs and check out the present I have for you on the bed?" Don came up behind her as she was taking in the breeze. She turned to look at him with a grin; she didn't even protest about him buying her anything. She followed his directions and went into the cabin master suite.

A smile crept on her face as she saw the box that had to be holding a dress. She quickly opened it! There was a beautiful, cream, off the shoulder dress, with gold stilettos and a strap that wrapped around her ankles. A note was lying on the bed,

"*This is the color you were wearing on our first date.*" She laughed at the thought of him remembering that.

She raced to the master bathroom, and there was a picture of her on their first date. She picked up the note that was lying on the counter, "*Wear your hair like you did on our first date.*" She smiled.

Doll then took her clothes off and jumped in the shower. There was another note attached to a body wash gift basket, "*On our first date, you had this*

intoxicating aroma about you, that was left on me, even after the date was over. I have a confession... I didn't take a shower that night because I wanted to sleep with your smell on me. Please wear it again."
She laughed at him. She shampooed her hair, left it in its natural curl state, and caressed her body with the body butter and perfume from the gift basket. She was ready to show her man what he had created.

She opened the door. A smile crept on her face, as gold rose petals and cream tea candles were guiding her way back to her man. Cautiously, she followed the petals and candles. It led to a circle of tea candles, with gold rose petals sprinkled in it. A cream, cashmere blanket, lay in the circle, with an assortment of chocolate covered strawberries, wine, and a mini chocolate fountain with a tray of different fruits.

She was amazed at the fact that he created something so beyond beautiful in 45 minutes. There was a note on the outside of the circle, *"Walk towards the rails and peer overboard, but clap your hands three times. Those three times represents the three years from our first date."* She strutted toward the edge, looked across the ocean, and there wasn't anything but darkness. Then, she remembered to clap three times. Clap! I Am Ready for Love by Indie Arie, soulfully filled the yacht. Clap! Fireworks went off over the boat. Clap! Candles she didn't see before, were floating in the water, next to a wreath of gold rose petals that spelled out, Will You Marry ME?

She was in reverence at the sight; tears welled up in her eyes. She turned around in search of him and saw him kneeling in the circle on one knee. Doll ran to him! She didn't know how she did it in those shoes, but she didn't stumble, nor slow down her steps.

There in their golden paradise, her man knelt, in all-cream attire, jacket, tie and cufflinks to boot. He went all out for this, she thought , as she held her hand out to accept the ring. "The ocean already asked you for me, but I want to ask you again." He pulled the ring out and placed it on the tip of her finger, "Will you marry me?" Doll actually hesitated for a second; it wasn't obvious to Don. The question is will he be faithful? Is he being faithful now? She looked down in his eyes and saw the love and sincerity in them. She couldn't say no to him; she couldn't say no to that face. "Yes, I would be honored." She told him.

Don loved Doll. She was fine, intelligent, clever, sexy, and witty and she liked sports. On top of all that, she could cook her ass off. She could get his dick hard just by the way she answered her phone. Baby Doll was everything to him. That is why he went through all this and was now down on one knee.

He admits it was hard work at first, getting her to open up. Getting Doll to depend on him in some places was hard; it was as if she couldn't trust anyone to lead. She was just used to handling shit on her own. Not just with taking care of herself financially, but with her emotions. All the anger and pain from her childhood, she held in. She dealt with the day-to-day stress herself, but she kept all that inside, in order to help him through his ordeals. Then there was the mental illness she was trying to

control. He thought it was fucked up what her father

did; he believed that the mental illness wasn't as bad

as she thought it was. She cared about his happiness

and he hers. He wasn't always on that page; it took

him some doing to get his whorish ways out of his

system.

The Wake-up

"Baby, we have to go to the emergency room! I'm bleeding," Doll scared Don out of his sleep. Doll was holding her four-month pregnant stomach, with tears in her eyes. He could see the pain on her face; something was definitely wrong.

Don jumped up, scurrying to put his jogging pants on! Not caring about the blood, he picked Doll's ass up, and carried her out the house! Luckily for Doll, she had on pajama bottoms. It wouldn't have mattered to Don if she were ass naked; his mind was on getting her to the hospital. Trying his best to zigzag through the morning traffic, Don looked over at Doll. Doll, still in pain, was rubbing Don's leg to comfort the both of them. They didn't want to think about what was happening to their first unborn child. They didn't dare think negative; they both were still holding onto a strand of hope.

"Baby? You alright over there?" Don asked as he reached down to squeeze her hand.

"I'm good. Just turn on the radio," she said, as another pain shot threw her body. She needed something to just take her mind off of what she knew was happening with their baby.

"Don, I stopped taking the medicine when I found out I was pregnant. Do you think I-"

"NO," he cut her off, knowing exactly what she was going to say. Don raised her hand up to his mouth and kissed it, "I love you Doll Baby," he told her as he held their eye contact. It was a look to reassure her that, no matter what happens, he loved her. Doll gave him a weak smile, "I love you too."

At that moment, Doll knew that he wouldn't love her any less for losing his baby. Don turned the radio on to the morning show; they were bound to get some laughs out of them.

The radio personalities.... "Wow! Cheerleaders and players are not supposed to mess around. Why can't these league players get this in their heads? DON'T MESS AROUND WITH THE CHEERLEADERS, THE GROUPIES, AND YOUR TEAMMATE'S MOM!" Laughter erupted in the studio, and even Doll and Don chuckled at the last remark. "So, how many players does the Colts Cheerleader have on her subpoena list?" one of them asked. "FIVE!" "FIVE!" they all said in unison. "She could have called Maury for that shh..." "Naw, VH1 is going to do a show called Jump-off's of the NFL!" "Lord, you just gave them an idea!" "She didn't learn shh from Evelyn; messing with an NFL player will get you head butted." Laughter erupted again.

Doll looked at Don and he shrugged his shoulders like, 'Shit... this is the first I'm hearing about this.' Plus, he was saying in his head, 'I strap up.' These thirsty broads weren't about to catch him slipping. He did too much to get Doll, and he wasn't about to throw that a way.

"Who's on the list?" "Let's see, we got the ladies' man Jeremiah Thompson, Rico "Suave" Espinoza,

Daniel Turner, Christian Malone and all-time favorite, Donovan Paine. All of them players for the Indianapolis Colts."

Doll's whole body went numb... Donovan Paine was like a loud ass echo that paralyzed her whole body and everything else that was said on the radio was no longer audible. It seemed as if the pain of her miscarriage became worse, her head was spinning, and something in her wanted to lash out and fuck Don up. At that time, blood started running down her legs, onto the hand she had sitting between her thighs.

Don was on ten! Who in the hell leaked that type of information? He didn't even know about it. It had to be that white blond bitch or was it the red head? He thought they would play their fucking part and he knew he wore a condom. There was no way in hell he was going to bring something back to Doll or his baby. "DAMN!" he shouted, and hit the steering wheel, "Doll Baby, I - "

She smacked the rest of the words right out of his mouth, and couldn't stop lashing out at him, "DOLL BABY," Smack, "MY," Smack, "ASS," Smack,

"MOTHER FUCKER!" Here she was having a miscarriage, and now it was national news that he might have gotten a bitch pregnant. Don couldn't do anything but try to block her hits. A pain shot through Doll that was so unbearable she wailed out like a banshee. Don threw open his car door and ran to her side, to carry her out.

"How could you do this to me?" she screeched in pain, as he picked her up and carried her into the hospital.

"Baby, I'm sorry! I love the fuck out of you! I never wanted to see you hurt." Don protested, as he carried her pain stricken body and heart through the emergency doors.

They immediately took her back because of the amount of blood she was losing. The nurse looked at him and gave him some wet wipes and alcohol pads, with a suspicious look. Puzzled at her disdained look, like she knew what was going on. Finally, Donovan felt the stings from the scratches and the wet stickiness on his face. He put his hand on his face, and red residue was on his hands when he pulled it down. "What the fuck," he said. Praying that no cameras were around to see him in this state, he swiftly went to the men's bathroom.

Reality just hit his ass, as he saw the blood on the wipe! This was the blood of his unborn seed. The woman that he loves is losing their child, and to add insult to injury while losing it, she finds out he might have a child on the way, by some jump off cheerleader.

The anger of his stupidity overtook him! He looked at the man in the mirror, and couldn't help but punch him…. punish him. The mirror shattered all around him; showing him only pieces of his distorted reflection. Don shed a couple of tears with his head *in his hands. He fucked up! Damn and he fucked up this time severely.*

This last year he had grew-up, especially after the scare he had. To see his Doll Baby hurt like that was enough to kick his heart in his throat. She didn't speak to him for 6 months... until the scandal was over. It was the worst 6 months of his life. He decided that if she stuck with him through that and forgave him, he would change, and he had. It was time for him to do grown man things and make her his wife.

This was the moment of no return; the time to see what her man was made of. I mean three years, a paternity scare, a miscarriage and the groupies. Oh, she deserved this moment! She deserved this moment a long time ago as she watched her man grin from ear to ear at her vibrant, yet hesitant, yes!

She wondered was he ready for this or was it just that he thought he would lose her, if he didn't take the next step. Was he through with letting the fame and money go to his head, the partying, the groupies, and the cheerleaders? It had been a year and a half since they'd been in the situation where he was caught cheating. She knew what she could be up against when she met the college football star at a college mixer. Did he really change, or did he get better at hiding it? How was she supposed to know for sure?

They both decided to stop dwelling in the past, as they sat, drinking wine and enjoying the beauty of each other and this moment. That wasn't all that was up Donovan sleeves. After the third glass of wine, "No more," he told her seductively. Donovan pulled his dreads back into a ponytail. He clapped once; the music changed and a sensual seductive melody started to play, as Don completely undressed himself. Doll took in her well-sculpted and chocolate all over man. He was blessed with the tools of a man that could satisfy a woman and give her an after glow. Once undressed, like it was timed, he gestured for her to stand. As he got on his knees, the words of the music started, *If you look this good.... I wonder how it tastes.*

Don licked his way up her thighs... pulling the hem of her dress up along with him. Reaching her yoni, he gently sunk his teeth into it. Doll shivered and let out a moan as he buried his face deeply into her. *Baby if I touch your body.... hear you scream my name.* He pulled her panties down with his teeth and was back up in a flash, to pull her dress up over her head.

Now, she was fully naked, with only her stilettos on. Her golden skin complimented the gold rose petals and cream candles. It was as if she were meant to be in this setting. *Would you whisper... to... me ... it's yours?* Now on his feet, he glides behind Doll, with his manhood pressed against her bounteous behind, and he moves their body to the hypnotic sounds of Jeremiah's 5 senses. *Girl you smell so gentle & pure... you controlllll, my senses.* He bends his neck to bite the back of her neck, as he rubs his hands down the curves of her body. *Babyy alllll my senses.* Feeling as if her body was on fire, longing for more of him, Doll tried to turn around to face him. He quickly turned her back around and smacked her on her

27

ass. The smack on her ass was to let her know he was in control, so she let him lead.

If you look this good.... I wonder how it taste. Baby if I touch your body.... He grabbed her hand and led her closer to the chocolate fountain, assortment of fruits and the chocolate covered strawberries. *Hear you scream my name. Would you whisper... to... me ... it's yours?* Seductively, he laid her beautiful body down... *Girl you smell so gentle & pure... you controlllll my senses...baby all of my senses.* He grabbed two cherries, dipped them in the chocolate, and placed them on her nipples. It was a wet, but pleasant feeling. She smiled from ear to ear, in anticipation for what he was going to do next. Doll felt her nipples harden. She bit her bottom lip, as Don came toward her, with a chocolate strawberry, leaving a trail from her left thigh, to the middle of her stomach, and up between her breast; each touch in sync with the music. *Would you whisper... to... me ... it's yours?*

He traced the strawberry around her lips, urging her to bite into it. She took the whole thing into her mouth and bit down. The surprise of the coconut Ciroc even made her bite her bottom lip seductively. That was what they took shots of on their first date. *You controlllll, my senses.* He moved the tip of his tongue across her lips, tasting the coconut, chocolate, and strawberry juices, that covered her lips. *Babyy alllll my senses. He* kissed her deeply, sucking in her tasty tongue. He winked at her as he kissed his way to the cherries on her nipples, licking and devouring them until the chocolate and cherry were gone. *You control my senses-* "*MMMMM*" Doll's moan was like music to his ears.

Not waiting another moment, he took a grape and put it in his mouth rolled it over her clit, the coldness of the grape made her arch her back. He knew he had her, he could see her yoni juices running down her upper, inner thighs. He licked it up and commenced to use the grape on her clit with his fingertips and his mouth to satisfy one of his senses and she tasted good like always. Probing his tongue in and out of her opening

29

while making circles with the grape on her clit, took
her to heights of a seductive vocal pitch, that Mariah
Carey would had to stop and listen to it.

Doll blessed his face with her womanly nectar, her
body thrashed around as if she were having an out of
body experience. She tried to move him but he clamped
down on her thighs and continued to torture her body
until she was out of breath in complete ecstasy.
Panting, she didn't utter a single word and neither
did he, no words were needed between them, no words
could explain this moment between them. They only
needed each other's body to know what the other
craved.

He popped the grape in his mouth. Don was full of
surprises, she watched as he stood up and produced a
bottle of warming massage oil. He spread it all over
his body, she started to protest and damn she wanted
the pleasure of rubbing that oil on every inch of his
chocolate body. He put his lips up to his mouth to shh
her. He made eye contact with her as he stroked his
penis to its full massive length. She salivated over

30

his glistening body and the slow way he stroked his manhood. Doll shook her head damn that man knew he was the shit, but it was cool she was the shit too.

He threw her the oil. He wanted to watch her caress her body with it. She put the oil in the palm of her hands. She started at the beginning of her thighs, sensually going downwards to her calves. Don watched in complete admiration of his soon to be wife's body. The night sky and candles flickering around the deck made one hell of an atmosphere. Don took in the sight before him and couldn't stop stroking himself; his eyes followed her hands everywhere they went.

He was done being a voyeur. He wanted to be the one to touch her all over. Don pulled Doll up to her feet and they started kissing and touching each other savagely. Hungry sexual appetites made them forget their bodies were slippery. Don lifted her up and she wrapped her legs around him, he entered her with ease and the friction of their oily bodies glided against each other. Each upward thrust for him and downward movement for her were pure erotic bliss. Somehow

31

their animalistic craving for each other overtook them and their bodies moved frivolously, Don slipped and lost his footing and they both fell. Laughing at themselves, "OMG, my butt hurts," Doll laughed, rubbing her butt.

Donovan was still laughing; he couldn't believe himself. "I'm good. Thanks for breaking my fall, Mrs. Paine," he laughed.
"Oh, you got jokes? Just for that, I'm sitting out for the whole season. Doll joked and tried to roll from under him.
"Oh hell naw! I'm about to ta- dat- der ass up." He stopped her and inserted himself inside her. They made love until they exhausted the possibilities of making love. However, during the night, Doll realized she had to face reality; no matter how much she loved him. Could he stay faithful? It was something she had to find out before they said I do.

The Doubt

Doll wondered who she could tell the good news to. She didn't have any more relatives. She refused to get close to the football player's girlfriends and wives. Most of the people she talked to were business associates, writers, or Don's friends. She wanted to call her old roommate who grew to be a sister to her; tears welled up in her eyes. She flashed back to that weekend Shawna showed up unexpected.

College Campus

Envy strutted on Spelman's campus like she owned every blade of grass on it. She looked around as if all eyes would be on her, but the women of Spelman came from all walks of life. Envy wasn't anything special or uncommon to see where some of them were from, so she didn't make an impact like she thought she would.

"What up, Bitch?" Envy squealed with a little distaste in her voice when Doll opened the door.

The look on Doll's face looked as if she saw a bad memory come into place. Doll snapped out of it quickly, and greeted her old friend with a hug. "Hey, Shawna," Doll said opening the door for her to come in.

"Let me introduce you to my roommate, Jazmin," she walked her toward the kitchen where Jazzy was. Shawna's eyes became wide because Doll and Jazzy favored each other so much. "Jazzy, this is my girl Shawna from back home." She told her sitting down at the table.

"Hey, Girl," Jazzy said in a friendly way.

Envy didn't like that shit, she sensed that now her position in Doll's life was overshadowed by her little copy look alike ,and why the fuck was she so damn cheerful, Envy thought?

"What's up, Girl? So who has the paid boyfriend or the rich daddy because I don't see many college girls living like this?" Envy said sitting on the one of the stools next to the breakfast bar. Her eyes took everything in…. These two bitches were living better than her, and she was a headliner, and dug in many of pockets and safes, she might add. Doll shook her head undetected by Envy, to let Jazzy know not to say anything.

The truth was that Doll ran away from Gary after working in the strip club for two weeks. Envy had tricked Doll into stripping for an old man. She basically pulled off while Doll was already stripping, thinking she was getting something out the car. She continued to strip for this old White man and once, Doll started swinging around the pole and playing with her pussy.

The old man pulled out a briefcase filled with money and gave it to her, "If you let me taste your pussy from the back, you can have this briefcase full of money. I'm about to die anyway, I just want one last thrill. Don't worry; it's nothing you could catch. " he told her. She looked at the briefcase, and thought damn she could quit this shit altogether and go straight to Spellman like she planned on doing in a year.

She bent over and let that old man go to work, he was adequately good at it too. It helped that he was a nice looking older man. He didn't even look that old to be dying, but you never know. When they were done, she went to the bathroom to freshen up and put her clothes back on. While putting on her shoes, she heard a bang. She raced out to find the man lying dead with a fist sized hole in his head. It wasn't the first time she saw a scene like this, so she didn't scream. She just took all the money out of the briefcase, put it in her bag with her costume, and got the fuck up out of there... Out of the hotel room and out of Gary with 200,000 thousand dollars!

Now here she was almost three years later and in her last year of College as an English Lit Major.

Jazzy spoke up, "That would be me with the rich daddy."

"Umpf, figures," Envy said rolling her eyes.

Envy opened up one of her bags and pulled out a DVD," Jazzy why don't you pop this in," she told her in amused tone. She was about to show Doll's new best friend what was really hood about her.

"OMG, Baby Doll is that you? " Jazzy screamed from the living room.

Doll looked at Envy and shook her head. Envy smiled a triumphant smile. She didn't like how chummy Doll and her roommate were. She thought that this would alter "Jazzy's "image of Doll. Besides…. how dare she call her Baby Doll? That was her nickname for her since they were nine years old.

37

Envy's face must have dropped to the floor when Jazzy was imitating Doll's every move, "So, this is when you were The Golden Doll, I see why girl, that gold hair, gold skin and those moves! You make all those other bitches look raggedy." She laughed. Doll laughed to herself; she knew Envy was steaming.

This bitch, ugh, she felt like she needed to break up their friendship. Envy looked at Jazzy; she was into the video like it was a step by step guide to working it like a stripper. She was moving and booty popping, which gave her an idea, "So, I know these college boys in the ATL got money. You down to strip, Jazzy, and see how your girl, The Golden Doll, used to get down?" She said with a devious smirk on her face.

If looks could kill, Envy would be dead right about now, "OMG, Really, I always wanted to show my naughty side!" Jazzy stated giggling, as she popped her booty in the air.

Envy jumped up and said, "See, that's the shit I'm talking about right there. Let's turn these college boys out. We can have a strip party right here. We three can be the only one's getting money." Envy started booty popping right along with Jazzy.

"Shawna let me holler at you for minute." Doll walked in her room and Envy followed.

"What the fuck do you think you doing? You not slick! You didn't come to see me. You came so I can help you make money. Or your ass is running from some nigga you stole from. Wait or is it both? You are not about to pull me in your bullshit and you most definitely not pulling Jazzy in none of your ghetto ass theatrics. That girl is not about that life. She is sheltered and she doesn't need to be corrupted." Doll snapped.

"Oh snap, crackle, and fucking pop! You came all the way here and grew some balls. Whatever, that bitch grown and if she wants to be about that life, I'm for damn sure going to show her that life and make my

fucking money too. So you can't talk me out of shit,
you better try to stop -"

Jazzy ran in with her stripping outfit, "Look! I got
just the outfit!" she said, grinning from ear to ear,
holding up a red see through thong set.
Envy started fanning herself and whispered, "Oops too
late…. Envy wins again. You better tag along to make
sure I don't turn her into a big money hungry ho." She
laughed as she sashayed out to prepare for the private
party that she already set up. "Ah Jazzy, let me show
you how to clap those cheeks with no hands." Then just
to annoy Doll, she started singing, 'Bands will make
her dance.'

Doll set in the car that night. If Jazzy wanted to
follow behind Envy, fine. Like Envy said, she's grown.
Envy was like a predator and anyone she could get over
on, she would make them her prey. Doll went along for
Jazzy's sake. She was thinking how sweet of a girl
Jazzy was, and she was the only female she has been
close to besides Envy.

Jazzy was a good girl from a small city in North Carolina. She had a 3.9 GPA and was going to school to become a doctor. It was uncanny how they favored each other, except for the color of their hair. Doll had sandy brown hair and Jazzy's was black. She just started dating this guy from Morehouse name Bone; she calls him a square, but she loves him. Doll never met him, nor has Jazzy met her man, Don. Jazzy had become her best friend over the year since she's been her roommate. Next weekend they were going to get their men together to finally meet each other since they were both Morehouse men. Doll was looking forward to having a normal kind of life without all the bullshit.

Envy came out the motel room and down the stairs to smoke whatever she was smoking. Doll was pissed and got out the car, "What the fuck you leave her in there for?" She said walking toward her.

"Damn she cool! She's already a pro and don't worry, she isn't doing anything but dancing-"

"Aaaaaaaaaaaaahhhhhhhhhhhhhhhh! Leave me alone," they heard Jazzy scream from upstairs. Doll was the first

41

one up there with Envy behind her. They busted in the room to find the dudes trying to rape her.

Doll pulled out her gun, "Listen mother fuckers! Back the fuck up off of her and I won't shoot your dicks off." The men stopped and instead of raising their hands, they grabbed their dicks.

Envy laughed, "For you guys to be College boys, you mother fuckers are stupid. She still can shoot your dicks off! Your hands aren't doing shit." She went to go through their pockets and pick the money up off the floor.

Jazzy got up quickly and grabbed her clothes. She was shaken up and terrified, she was not about this life and she never wanted to be. She should have listened to Doll. She even dyed her hair the same as Doll's. Her Korean mother was going to kill her.

"Man look… shit just got out of hand…My bad, but you need to tell ol' girl to give us back our money and shit." One said.

Envy laughed when she went to a pair of pants that had shit in there that resembled a drug dealer, "Oh, we got ourselves a hustler, ladies," she said pulling out a wad of money wrapped with rubber bands.

"If you knew what was best for you, you'll forget you even saw that shit and put it back in my pocket," stated the guy who seemed to be the only man not sweating bullets about being held at gunpoint. The hustler was pissed. All he came to do was drop off some X for these college boys; he knew he should have told him to meet him downstairs, but when he came in and saw Jazzy and Envy, he wanted to watch the show.

"Charge that shit to the game," Envy told him.

He charged at Envy, and automatically Doll let off. Pandemonium broke out, someone flicked the lights off, and the boys ran naked, with clothes in their hand, out of the room. The girls ran, all but Doll, she had to find the casing. It was lying next to the hustler; she bent down to pick it up. The hustler grabbed her

43

by her wrist, "This shit ain't over bitch, I will find you." he told her as he coughed up blood.

"You can come to G.I. if you want to mother fucker. But you won't make it out." Doll told him as she yanked her arm away from him. She wiped off her fingerprints from the doorknob; she didn't have time to wipe down anything else. One thing she can say was that at least Envy was smart enough to go two hours away from the ATL.

The hustler had already took the liberty of snapping Doll's picture and sent it to his cousin and boss, Bone.

Bone did a double take as he high-tailed it to the motel where his cousin said he was. "What the hell? It was too late. His cousin sent it to him and his goons. The girl in the picture looked identical to his girlfriend Jazmin, but with blond hair. He wondered was that the surprise hair color she wanted to show him when she texted him. Naw, that can't be her, he *said to himself, stripping for some random niggas at a motel. Can't be her!*

When Bone reached the motel, cops and medics were everywhere. He didn't have to go upstairs; his cousin was in the ambulance already, with a sheet over him. Bone did the cross sign. He was going to fuck his frat brothers up and find the chick that killed his cousin. His cousin said the bitches said they were from G.I., as if G.I. was a no man's land. The only G. I. he could think of was the murder capital, Gary, Indiana. He didn't care where they were from; they bleed just like the rest of the world.

Bone high tailed it out of there on a mission; he had tears running down his face. Somebody was going to tell him something and soon. He had one more year of being a Morehouse man, equipped with knowledge, gangster and ambition. He was ready to take the world and the underworld by storm as an Investment Banker.

His cousin's death was the only thing occupying his mind that he forgot to tell his boys to hold off on finding that female.

Back at Doll's

Jazzy had just came out of her bedroom from e-mailing and texting Bone. Still shook up about the ordeal, she jumped at every sound. Doll came to give her a sympathetic hug, while Envy rolled her eyes. Envy felt like it was over and now they needed to move on… Jazzy wanted to be about that life, so she needed to put her big girl thongs on. Envy sat there and counted the money, "10 g's? What the hell was he doing carrying 10 g's around?"

"10 g's! They are coming back for that! You better hope and pray that this shit don't come back on Jazzy and me. We are the ones that live in this city! You get to crawl back to the G." Doll told her.
Envy noticed a different side of Doll. Questions swarmed in her head, but fuck that! She had 10 g's! She can act brand new if she wanted to.

46

"Look, I have to go see Don! You two," she said
pointing to Jazzy and Envy," *Stay low."*
She needed to clear her head she probably just killed
a man; her whole future was at stake.
*"Girl, she is tripping! You know what I'm just going
to go ahead and leave. I have caused enough trouble.
Do you mind taking me to the bus station, Jazzy?"* Envy
asked.
"Maybe, we should wait for Doll-"
*"Naw, do you see how pissed she is? Believe me…. I
know Doll. It's best I leave now before she gets
back."*
"Okay," She grabbed her keys.
"Look," Envy said grabbing three g's, *"Here"* I'm sorry
for everything. I didn't know those college boys were
going to be like that."* Jazzy grabbed the money and
put it on the table. Maybe Envy wasn't that bad after
all.
Heading to the Greyhound Bus station proved to be the
worst mistake of Jazmin's young life. Coming back, she
was gunned down by masked men.

Doll couldn't function during the funeral, but she did see a man staring at her like she was a ghost. Like he knew she should have been the one in that casket…..

After that, she never spoke to Shawna again. She left school; bought a condo in Nap, and here she was three years later wishing she had a friend to share her moment with, so she called Envy anyway!

"Girl, get out of here." Envy said out of shock.

"Yes, girl! I'm engaged!" She was happy, but yet still hesitant, but it didn't show in her voice.

"Wait…Is this the same dude that was cheating with groupies and shit?"

"Yeah," Doll told her reluctantly.

"The same dude that had to go to court because one of those cheerleaders claimed he was the father?" Envy asked out of spite.

"And, what are you getting at Shawna?"

"I'm just saying, how you know you can trust him? I mean, it is not like you didn't have proof. Shit, the whole world had proof when he had to take the DNA test and admitted to sleeping with ol girl."

"All that shit is behind us now; it's been about two years since that incident. We've been going strong since."

"How do you know he's not cheating on you right now? Girl you are so naive when it comes to men. Once a cheater, always a cheater just ask Oprah, Tyra and Dr. Phil, whoever, and they will tell you the same shit. That is why I will never let these men get the best of me. I replace these men once I get that money out of them. Yo ass went to College and forgot all about what I taught you!"

"Whatever, people can change," Doll said with a little less confidence than she had before.
"I tell you what, I got a plan. I'll come down this week and tell you." This conversation couldn't have come at a better time. Envy needed a different breed of sponsors; these street hustlers weren't getting it

for her. She rolled her eyes thinking about the way Jah played her.

"I don't know about all that. Tell me what you got in mind first. I remember the last time you came to visit me, some shit popped off."

"Okay," Envy said rolling her eyes, "Does Don know what I look like?"

"No."

"Cool, I'll come down, you can tell me where he's going to be, and I'll see if he'll cheat or if he's a changed man. If he has changed, then no harm, no foul, but, if he takes the bait, then you know what type of nigga you getting." Envy told her. She was pleased with her own plan, as she just visualized bursting this bitch's bubble.

Doll became quiet.

"Look, Baby Doll, I'm only thinking of you. You don't want to marry this man if you're gonna always be wondering if he is going to be faithful. No female wants to live like that. I know you all in love and shit, so I know his money doesn't matter to you. Shit, if you were a chick like me, you'd say fuck it and marry his ass anyway because NFL wives are done lovely. Besides, how is he going to find out we know each other? I mean, if he cheats, he is not going to say anything and if he doesn't, I can just say it was a coincidence that we know each other.

"Fine, I'll see you next week. By the way, how in the hell are you going to spend a whole week down here? Aren't you going to be missing out on Dollar's money?" "Don't worry about it," she snapped, "I need to get from up here anyways, get a change of scenery, and come kick it with my home girl." She said as she rolled her eyes.
"Alright. Bye."
"Bye!" Envy added.

She needed an opportunity to get out of town. Also she hadn't saw Doll since she worked at the strip club for two weeks and went off to college.

These niggas act like they can't just charge it to the game any more. Shit, they knew her rep. She was known for shaking a niggas pockets, involuntarily or voluntarily. She felt like somebody should have told that nigga, Jah, that if he were attached to his money, he shouldn't have fucked over ENVY. Envy had introduced Jah to Shawna, the woman, not Envy Me, the stripper. So what that nigga was locked-up and now she had his dope money. He shouldn't have left it at her crib. Who in the hell does that, especially since she found out she wasn't his main girl.

Besides, she already spent half of it and she needed new gear. She called it her "Catch a Baller Gear." From what she heard, he would be out soon and his people were already looking for her, so she knew it was time to bounce. If she were going to draw the attention of a NFL Football player, she knew she had to change her look from ghetto fab to just fab. More of Jah's money was going to get invested into her new venture. She knew Doll's style. Doll was sophisticated and sexy, without even trying too hard.

It was time to go shopping and get a un-stripper-fied makeover.

Envy strutted out of her grandmother's basement; oblivious to her surroundings. She figured no one knew where her grandmother lived because she lived in Calumet City. She would be wrong; Jah watched her as she left the house.

Jah shook his head at the carelessness of the chick he once deemed his match on the criminal side of things. He wanted her on his team to conquer his plan, but the test he gave her proved her to be disloyal. He knew having his cousin call her was pushing her to the limit, especially with his cousin acting as if she were his main chick. He didn't treat her like a jump off; he treated her and introduced her to a lifestyle she wasn't accustomed to. He treated her to the life of a lady, opened her doors for her, brought her flowers, wined and dined her, made love to her, and fucked her when she needed to be fucked. Her guard was completely down for him and that's when he went in for the kill. He liked fucking her, spending time

53

with her, but he wanted someone else, someone to him that was a replica of someone he loved.

Envy went on about her business shopping at River Oaks Mall, never paying attention because she felt believed she was safe. She brought expensive luggage, outfits, shoes, accessories; she didn't spend too much because she wanted to leech of Doll's wardrobe. Doll's attire was upscale compared to what Envy could afford; she hated that siddity ass bitch. Especially that night four years ago, when Envy invited herself down to her college campus. Thinking back on the present she wouldn't have fucked with Jah so intensely if that nigga Dollar didn't mess up...

Jah

Entering Black Cherries, all eyes were on him. The women were trying to figure out whom new money was and the main line hustlers were giving him respect and wondering why he was there. The flashing lights in the club hit his stones just right. It was as if rays of light were coming from parts of his body where his jewelry laid. Jah wasn't really into being flashy or strip clubs, but he was on a mission. He gave a few hustlers head nods and kept it moving until he found what he was looking for. At first glance, you would think Jah was a street hustler. Jah "Bone" Mabon was a hustler, but a legit hustler. He was an Investment Banker and he had illegal clients, as well as legal clients. He was a Morehouse man that knew how much illegal money was made in the hood and he chose to do business in Gary, Indiana, Chicago and Indianapolis for a reason.

There she was, the girl he wanted, chocolate, with the right face and right body. While dudes were running to the stage to see the headliner, Envy Me, they called her. Jah stood at a distance peeping her every move. When he caught her staring at him while she swiveled her pussy on some random dude's face, he took off his sunglasses and stared right back at her. The look was intense; he could tell he had her undivided attention. She gestured for him to come to her, he put his sunglasses back on and walked away. Envy felt disrespected. No man has ever turned her down, but she was also turned on by him. She had to find out who he was and fast. He might be the one to take her out of the strip club. She could tell he was winning and she wanted to be in the winning circle.

After the Club

Envy called Dollar as she was leaving the club. Now, Dollar was the exception to some of her rules. He was a street hustler that didn't mind spending money on a chick, so she made him her main ATM . He was hers and no other bitch was allowed to take up his time, if she wanted it. By no means was any bitch from Black Cherries supposed to get up on him. It was a deadly rule she made clear to all those Monday morning stripping ass females. She was the headliner…What she says goes and it helped that Dollar was Co-owner of the club. After being with the mysterious fine man without him even trying to engage in any sexual activity, she needed a pick me up and a dick me down.

Dollar was just the man she needed to boost back up her ego.

"Hey, Where are you?" she asked once he answered the phone.

"Handling some business. I'll get up with you when I'm done, Shorty." Dollar said into the phone
"Okay, don't have me waiting all night. You know how impatient my pussy gets."
"Yeah, you better not be giving my shit away."
"Come get it and then I won't. Don't get it twisted I don't give shit away! "She told him and hung up the phone

She had a smile on her face as her phone started ringing. She looked at the screen, "Ha, umm! I knew that nigga would get right back to me." She answered the phone, "oh you-"

She was stopped dead in her tracks as she heard what sounded like one of the strippers from the club in the background. She didn't utter another word. She just

57

listened; it was obvious that Dollar's phone called her back.

"Ummm... Dollar, you know I've been waiting for you to give me some of this," she said between what sounded like slurps.

"Shut up and just suck my dick. I need to go chill with my shorty." Dollar informed her.

It sounded as if the girl stopped giving him head, *"Why in the hell you mess with that grimy ass ho? I heard that bitch made one of your girls turn tricks at gunpoint, had about 20 niggas piss on her and then she took all of that girl's money. She even made the girl walk home butt naked without taking a shower while she drove along on the side of her laughing. "* She protested.

Listening on the other end, Envy shook her head," *A snitching ass bitch… Now that's that shit I don't like, and besides it was only 10 dudes,"* she laughed to herself.

Dollar laughed loudly, "If that bitch was stupid enough to let her, then so be it. I don't knock my shorty's hustle and she doesn't knock mine. So either put that dick in your mouth or get the fuck out my crib."

She must have obliged his command because Envy heard slurping again.

Envy hung up the phone, drove to Dollar's crib, and used her key. She crept into the room, and low and behold, it was that new bitch Butter, getting her head game on ruthlessly. She easily slipped back out of the room and went straight to Dollar's safe. Dollar was so full of himself that he didn't lock his safe up when he was home. He thought nobody was dumb enough to try him while he was there. She filled her bag up with stacks of hundreds and a bag full of X pills, and dipped back out to her car. Silently, she put it in her trunk, checking her surroundings to see if anyone were out at 3am in the morning. The vicinity was clear, so she crept back into the house with her gun *in her hand. When she arrived, undetected once again, she made sure to make her presence known.*

She cocked her gun, "Ah, Can I join you?" she pointed the gun at them.

Dollar wasn't scared and didn't even move to cover himself up or remove his penis from her mouth. Butter on the other hand, was scared as hell. She heard what this chick was capable of and she wanted no parts of it.

"Don't be scared! I'm not mad! I just want to have a little fun." She reassured Butter.

By this time, Butter ceased her oral skills and sat up in the bed, wondering what the hell Envy was going to do to her.
Still pointing the gun, Envy stripped down to her chocolate bare skin and walked toward the bed. Butter tried to get out the bed…. Envy grabbed her by her weave and put the pistol up to her head. "No, if you

fuck one of mines, you have to fuck with me." She told her.

"Besides I just want to have some fun, she told her, tracing the barrel of the gun around her nipples. She forced her down on the bed and placed her mouth on the breast that was traced by the gun. Envy tooted her bootie up, and Dollar knew she wanted it in her third hole.

Manhood still hard and swinging, he got behind Envy, while Envy placed her harden nipples in front of Butter's mouth, "You can partake, "Envy told Butter as she gestured with the gun towards her breast. She placed Envy's breast in her mouth, grabbing both and squeezing them together, enabling her to devour them both at the same time.

Dollar entered her, grinding it in with ease, to loosen the tight space up stroke by stroke. Envy loved every bit of his deep stroke and the look on this scared bitches face. She slowly moved the gun down to Butter's clit, rubbing the cold steel against her

61

flesh. The look on her face was priceless. Dollar

looked to the side to see what she was doing. He

laughed and smacked her on the ass, "OOO, THAT'S WHY I

FUCKS WITH YOU!" he busted off inside of her. He

pulled out of her still semi hard; quickly Envy

grabbed the girl by her neck and shoved the gun into

her mouth. She maneuvered herself off the bed, taking

Butter with her. "Yo baby! Sit on the edge of the

bed." She told Dollar as she yanked the girl down on

her knees face to face with Dollar's penis.

"You like my man's dick don't you?" she asked her as

she bobbed her head up and down for her.

"You like talking shit about me, don't you?" she

didn't wait for her to answer she made her do the

bobble head again.

"Now, since you like my man's dick and you let shit

about me come out of your mouth, she pressed the gun

to the girls temple, now, suck my shit of his dick."

She laughed

Butter eyes widened, as if Envy had lost her fucking

mind. She wasn't sucking this nigga's dick after he

had it all up in her ass. But , when she saw her turn

the safety off and heard her cock the gun, she started

licking that nigga like a lollipop.

After Dollar ejaculated for the second time empting

his seeds in the girl's mouth, she made sure she

didn't let an ounce fall from her mouth.

"Now," Envy said to her as she threw her clothes at

her, "Your services are no longer needed. I take it

you can see your way out."

Butter haven't moved or dressed so quickly in her

life. Envy stopped her from jetting out the door,

"Damn girl! Go and at least rinse out your mouth with

some mouthwash. The bathroom is down the hall and then

you are dismissed."

Dollar set back and lit up another blunt with

satisfaction written on his face, "You mad, Envy?" he

asked with a grin on his face.

"Yeah, I'm mad. Not because you had another broad in

here, but the fact that you canceled me to fuck with

one of the Monday night strippers. Hell Yeah I'm mad,"

she told him as she snatched the blunt from his hand.

"You spending the night?" he asked her, grinning at her theatrics.

"Yeah, I have to start keeping an eye on you. Let's go take a shower." She told him.

That night, she slept like a baby. That morning, Dollar was crying like a baby.

Envy made sure to raise Dollar's suspicion toward Butter; she anonymously sent the girl three thousand and to a Monday stripper, that is a lot of money that she didn't have to work for. She planted the pills in the girl's locker. That would teach her not to cross Envy. As expected, she flashed that shit around the club and went on a shopping spree. Dollar took notice, checked Butter's locker, discovered the pills, and sent his squad after her. All Envy knew is that she turned up dead in a dumpster on 5th avenue.

After that, she stopped messing around with Dollar. He had broken one of her rules. "Thou shall not put any chick before Envy." Now, it was time to get on the *mission of finding out who in the hell old dude from*

the club was.

Jah

"I heard you've been asking around about me." He said

to Envy, catching her off guard. He pressed his body

up against hers and sandwiched her between him and the

bar.

Envy was at a loss for words. The electricity that she

felt was undeniable. She had no words for this man,

now that they were face to face.

"So, now that I'm here, what do you plan to do with

me?" he teased, pinching her nipples through her

bikini top. Fire shot through her legs and from then on she was hooked.

All Envy could muster up was a blank stare. He chuckled, "What's your name?"

She found her voice," Envy Me, Envy for short," she told him pointing to her tattoo above her panty line.

"No, wicked girl! What's your real name… not your stripper name?" He asked as he bites her bottom lip. He stared her completely in her eyes, and she found it hard to turn away.

"Shawna," she told him. She was ashamed that not many men who came through the strip club asked her for her real name. Shit, everyone knew her name in there.

She let all her rules go, until he disappeared for a couple of months, leaving her sick, love sick. A woman like Envy didn't like putting her feelings into a man, but this time she fell and she fell hard. She thought he would be the one to take her out the strip club,

66

the one to wife her and give her everything her heart desired.

She started hearing rumors that he was in jail for possession. Then the phone calls came and an unknown woman called her about picking up Jah's money. The female didn't say she was his sister, cousin or nothing; she just demanded to pick up his money. In her eyes, this had to be his main chick. What other reason would she have to call her demanding some shit if he didn't give her permission to do so? Envy wasn't budging on that, she put on her game face, put her feelings in check, and got ghost on them. But, she knew hiding in Calumet City wasn't going to keep her safe for long. The move she made was what Jah wanted. He wanted her to lead him to her stripper partner. He liked Envy's sex, but he craved the petite, golden girl he saw at the funeral that day. It was three girls at that party, but only two were still alive. He knew he had one of them, but he wanted the one who pulled the trigger and got his girl killed.

Indianapolis was just a hop, skip, and a jump from Gary. She will soon realize that there was nowhere Jah could not reach her because he was watching her every move.

Now arriving at Doll's residence from the airport, Envy was already jealous of what she saw so far.

Doll had a condominium, a BMW 2012, 7series and designer clothes. Not the middle class designer clothes or should she say the 'Hood Rich' designer clothes, like Red Monkey, True Religion, Black Label , Mecca ,etc. She didn't even wear the white hood rich clothes, such as Polo, American Eagle, Abercrombie , Aeropostale, etc. The clothes that we hood rich or want to be wears with the name plastered all over them, so a motherfucker would know that you were wearing name brand shit. She's talking about classy shit, that you can just look at them and know that it's that expensive stuff. Damn, it got her pussy wet just thinking about that whole lifestyle.

Doll also had money and was very generous; in Envy's head, it was only right that she take advantage of it.

Shit, she couldn't understand how Doll lucked up on a winner, and she was stuck with these petty as dope boys. In her eyes, she looked ten times better than Doll, because she had a body as well as looks. Don't get her wrong, Doll was pretty, and when Doll was at the strip club, she was the most sought after dancer. Envy had sex appeal; she walked sexy, dressed sexy, and talked sexy. Envy oozed sex from her hair follicles to her toenails. So, she knew why Doll was skeptical because once Don laid eyes on her, she just knew he wasn't going to resist her and everything Doll had will be hers…

Her Plan

Envy had been there for two days now and Don was due back from camp tomorrow. Now it was time to see what Mr. Football had going for himself. When they pulled up to the estate, and she does mean Estate, she couldn't believe her eyes. Why was this bitch still living in that condo, when she could be living in this miniature mansion? Envy just shook her head; she has to be one of the stupidest bitches she has ever come across, and she was still ghostwriting, instead of just laying back and taking all that a NFL football contract had to offer.

When they entered the foyer, she saw this huge picture of Doll and Don. *Oh my damn! This nigga was fine too; his body looked like he could pick you up and just fuck you without any support whatsoever... She saw him play football once, but that was, because she was stripping at a Playoff after party in Nap. Now, she wishes she would have paid closer attention.* "Mmm, this is going to be so much fun and I'm going to enjoy myself with every stroke," she cooed to herself.

"So, what time is he getting back tomorrow?"

"8:00 at night."

"So, I'll go ahead and get the suite at the Radisson tonight. That way I can already be in the vicinity of where he hangs out." She said anxiously.

"That's cool. Just call me after it doesn't go down."

Yeah, Envy, thought, I'm going to call you while his screaming my name.

* * *

Don and his boys were relaxing from camp. They had at least seven more weeks before the season started. So, drinks at the club, by The Radisson, were good because several of them were leaving to go home to their families in other cities. This was his chance to celebrate his engagement with his boys; surprisingly they were happy for him.

They all have met and chilled with Doll; she was like one of the boys, except they found themselves fantasizing about being with this one. She stood tall by Don's side, like Hillary did Bill and like Cookie did Magic. On top of that, she wasn't after his money; she was a ghostwriter for several New York Times' Best Sellers. He had to beg her to buy her that BMW, for her birthday. So, in their eyes, marrying Doll was a good look for him.

Laughing and enjoying life was the only thing on their agenda tonight, and of course taking in some eye candy. One sister in particular was alone sipping on a glass of white wine. Watching her lips kiss the glass at each sip, had all the guys sneaking glances her way. She was classy but sexy as hell ,and it was something about her that made her seem very naughty. She was dressed in an all-black Gucci wrap around dress, with Gucci 3 inch heels to match. Her jet black hair was in a nice full side bun, with a swoop slick in the front. On her ears, simple diamonds, that matched her bracelet and her anklet.

Envy knew she looked superb, she spent $800 on the dress, $350 on the shoes, but the jewelry was just Doll's way of knowing that she doesn't do anything for free. When she found out that Don came back with his boys, she came out her pocket with $300 to get two girls she met at the Mall to come and act like her friends.

Of course she picked them out of hundreds of girls at the mall. She knew those two were money hungry, but a little settle with their approach; they weren't bad on the eyes, either. She knew when she mentioned football players and their eyes danced, they were sisters of the all mighty dollar.

When the two girls addressed her at the bar, she gave the one name, China, a hug and they greeted each other like old friends. It's funny how money can make a motherfucker fake the funk. China looked like she could have been one of Kimora Lee's daughters all grown up. Now, Tora was a chocolate sister with china doll eyes and a Colgate smile that would make a blind man take notice. China rocked jeans and an off the shoulder black shirt with some Jimmy Choos.

Tora wore small pin striped shorts with a bustier to match, with black Christian Louboutins . "Damn," Envy thought in her head, "I picked the right ones for the job. Damn, I wonder if Bergdorf Goodman is missing some shit because those shoes look just like the ones in Doll's closet," and she knew these chicks couldn't afford them.

It was three of them and four men. Being unevenly
matched seemed even better for Envy. She could always
save the leftover one for later. She made a mental
note on which one that would be, before she gave the
girls the plan. "Look, the chocolate brother with the
dreads is mine for now and the light skinned one with
the green eyes, I want for later. So if you do get
with him, don't give him your number." She told them
with a try me look.

"That's cool because all of them fine, so we not
missing out on nothing." China said, ready to get her
hooks into some real money.
They sat for about 45 minutes, and even though all the
men were admiring them, none of them came over to
introduce themselves. Being fed up with waiting, Envy
decided to take the first move. "Can I get a bottle of
Roederer, Louis Cristal Champagne sent over there to
that table?" she asked the barkeep.

The bartender reached them before they were about to
get up. All the men's eyes shot at the beautiful girls
at the bar.

Each man sat back down and filled their glasses, not wanting to be rude. It wasn't often that they got the treatment of women buying them drinks. In their heads, money hungry chicks were not going to come-out-of-pocket to buy any man a drink. However, Envy was not your average sack chaser. When she needed to step her game up, she did. Besides, this was a long term investment. The way she would be living after this was over would be ten times better than having a little change to buy a bottle of that quality.

The men sent the bartender back over with an invitation. Envy turned around and smiled, "It is show time," she whispered in a smiling China's ear. All three of them strutted over there, as if they were on a runway. All the men licked their lips except for Don. Don't get him wrong, they were sexy, but they weren't worth fucking up his relationship with Doll. They were having a good time. No one was ready to call in the night. Sex was in the air and they wanted to smell it.

"Ah, we should get a game of pool, Envy finally said.

"All the places are closed. Damn, Chad paused, that would be a good idea." he glanced over at Don and Don knew what he was getting at. He was cool with it, because he didn't have any temptation to overcome. He knew he was the only one of his teammates that lived nearby, so why spoil his boys' fun.

"Shit, we can kick it at my crib and play pool." Don smirked at Chad, who now wore a Kool-Aid grin on his face.

Back at Don's House

Envy was still in awe over the house, so faking like she has never laid eyes on it was easy. Envy played it very cool at the bar, not getting into anyone in particulars face. Keeping a neutral distance from all four men left her open with options. Therefore, when she followed the host to the bar, no one really missed her presence.

"Can I help you with anything?" Envy asked with a sexy smile on her face. She took off her shoes purposely to show off her pretty toes and fresh pedicure. Wearing no stockings was a good look. She had big legs and a little oil was all she wanted to cover them up with.

 She noticed him sneaking peeks at her legs; at one point, he even licked his lips.

However, what Don was thinking as he looked at her was, "*I hope this broad got panties on. I would hate for my baby to sit in some nasty coochie juice.*" He only licked his lips because they were dry. Even if Envy knew that, she still would swear up and down he was feeling her.

"Sure, tell me what you would like to drink, first, then you can assist me in making Hennessey and cokes."

"Well, I'm kind of a white wine girl myself. Do you have any? She asked as she looked over his shoulder, looking for what she knew wasn't there. Doll already told her he keeps his wine in the basement's wine cellar.

"Yeah, but not here I will be right back." He smiled politely as he left to go get the wine.

Envy smiled to herself as she hurriedly poured everybody's Henn and Coke. She made his drink first to let it sit and walked the other ones to the rest of them. As she was coming back for the last of the drinks, Don was coming back up stairs.

"I took the liberty of making the drinks for you since you went out of your way to get my wine." She smiled and left right back out leaving his drink on the countertop. He poured her wine, and then brought it to the pool table. She watched as the men sipped on their drinks and Don on his MDMA and drink.

Of course the plan wasn't to drug him; she made that decision on her own. She knew she would have to do something to loosen him; he acted as if his Doll was right there in the same room. He kept his distance as he watched them talk shit and play pool, and once they started playing strip pool, he walked out. Envy followed. She watched him carefully walk to the living room. She knew the drug was getting to him. He was putting too much thought into walking. At one point, he even stumbled and had to hold onto the wall the rest of the way.

Beware/XXX The Underground Playgrounds

Don flopped down on the couch, thinking that because he hasn't drunk anything for so long, the alcohol had him on his ass and his dick kept getting hard. He grabbed the remote and put his hands unconsciously on his aroused dick. For some reason, a porno caught his eye, and the girl giving this dude a professional, made him visualize that it was Doll Baby and he. He stroked his manhood; it was now out of his jeans. He couldn't help it… His body had a sexual fire burning through it and Envy watched wanting to put it out for him.

DAMN he was bigger than any man she has been with, and she had been with plenty and all sorts. She knew why Doll was so gone over him; he was fine, had long money, he was hung like a horse and on top of that, he didn't mind spending it on his woman. Where had he been all her life, she thought. She slowly walked over; he watched, but couldn't stop his hand from stroking his dick. She did not approach him; she just watched him and licked her lips. She went to the bar and grabbed the white wine bottle, went back, and stood over him.

"Mmmmm... stroke it harder," she said seductively, and when he did, she poured some of the liquid onto his manhood, as he stroked. When the liquid hit his skin, the movement became slicker and wetter. His eyes rolled into the back of his head as he let out a moan. She wanted to put his beautiful dick into her mouth so bad that she almost came thinking about it. Just as she was about to fall to her knees and put her fellatio skills to use, he exploded. Don let out six weeks' worth of backed up semen.

He jumped up hurriedly, "My bad! I have to go change. Look, I am sorry I don't know what is wrong with me. This shit was wrong, I have a fiancée! Man… She'd kill me if she knew about this shit!" he told her as he left without any eye contact.

Don didn't know what was wrong with his state of mind. However, he knew he wasn't thinking clearly; his dick was trying to take control of his body. That is what got him in trouble the other times, thinking with his little head. He took off his clothes, put on a pair of boxers, and all of sudden, the room started spinning. He crawled to the bed and laid on his back. The room went around a few times, his heart was beating faster, and his dick was still hard. Then nothing!

Envy quietly walked up stairs to Don's bedroom. She found him lying on his back with his boxers on. Damn he looked sexy, "Ummmmm... I wonder," she said as she moved closer to see if he were still hard. She knew it! That's another reason her dumb ass couldn't leave him! She knew even without the drug, Donovan was the kind of man that could get back up with no problem. "But now, it's going to be allll mine," she said in a low growl, as she took off her dress with her crotch-less red panty set.

Meanwhile in a Condo near them

Doll was on her third shot of Patron, trying to do anything to numb her mind. She didn't want to think of what might be going on. Once she felt like changing her mind, she knew it was already too late. She went back and forth with herself, having a conversation, with her mom as the angel, and her dad as the devil, just sitting on her shoulder. She knew she wasn't supposed to drink with her Meds, but she couldn't stand the visions. "What if it is like this all the time," she thought. Maybe Shawna was right; she couldn't marry him. She would always wonder if he were still the same whore he used to be. She set in her mind that the only way she could trust him was to put him in front of temptation. She knew her girl wouldn't let her down and she believed she was the best person to get close to fucking him, but wasn't going to. She trusted her with all her secrets, even about her mother's illness.

She thought back to when Shawna beat this girl's ass because she came to school talking about Doll's mother.

"That's why yo mommy killed herself, because she was crazy and my mommy said your daddy said you got the same thing." She blanked out and the memories of that night started flashing in.

The night her mother died

Doll remembered it like it was yesterday. Those days, nights, weeks and months that led to her mother's death. Even the days, hours, and seconds were embedded *in her mind forever. It was the night before her 9th*

birthday. Her mother didn't come into her room to lie

beside her. This night, her father didn't give her any

Benadryl that he usually gave her to put her to sleep.

She didn't know why he gave it to her, but he did.

Doll saw her mother take medicine all the time and the

pills made her act different, like she was in a

trance…. she was in her own world. She heard her

father come in, so she eased out of bed, ready for him

to give her, her medicine for her so called allergies.

Doll peeked around the coroner in purple pj's with the

feet, gripping her stuffed sheep dog. She saw a woman

in the living room with a tight, short dress on and

tall shoes. She was primping herself in the full

length mirror, in the living room, as if she had

invaded their home plenty of times. Doll watched her

slide off her dress, well it was more like a shimmy

peel off type of thing; the dress was so tight. The

lady sat down on their sofa, in her underwear and

heels, and picked up their house phone, "Hey girl,"

"No", "At Vick's house", "Girl please! He doesn't

care… He makes that crazy bitch get out of her own bed

so we can fuck! He might as well divorce the crazy bitch and move me in."

Bang! The door to her parents' bedroom slammed shut. The lady quickly hung up the phone; as if she were never on it. Her father was anxiously looking for something, storming through each room looking through cabinets, drawers and closets. Finally, he decided to look in the basement in the bathroom, "Damn it!" he said running upstairs with what looked like an empty pill bottle.

"You need to get your shit and leave, Kat!" he told her looking toward the bedroom door.

Kat wasn't having it, "Baabyyyyy, come on! Let's just do what we do somewhere else." She slithered near him, still in her underwear and tall shoes.

"No girl! Get your shit on NOW AND LEAVE!" he raised his voice, trying to get her to fathom the urgency of the situation. He looked in the direction of the bedroom again. He didn't even see Doll watching the whole scene; he was too concerned about what woman would come out of that room and he knew it sure as hell wasn't going to be the doped up oblivious wife he usually ran over.

"Are you serious? You're going to let all of this, she bagged back from him to do a full spin, go to waste?" She slinked back over to him, fell to her knees, and before he could protest, inserted his manhood into her awaiting mouth. Doll not knowing what was going on, knew a couple of things at her young age: one, that woman was nasty, two, her father was not supposed to be doing this, and three, if her momma saw them, she knew it was going to be a problem.

Her father, caught up in the moment, didn't hear the bedroom door come open; neither did her hear her mother creep up behind them. Doll's eyes grew big as she saw what was in her mother's hand. It's as if her mother knew what was going on in her living room and came prepared.

With a very slow calculated voice, she heard her mother say, "So, this is what you do when she's weak-minded, on her Chlorpromazine mixed with the unauthorized Ambien you give her?" It was 2 am in the morning and her mother was fully dressed in a business suit and heels. Her tone was unrecognizable. This wasn't the docile, sweet mother she was used to. It was like she was someone else! This wasn't the simple-minded, weak, crazy bitch (her father always called her) her father beat on and ridiculed. "Who in the hell is this?" she probed as she bore her eyes into the woman on her knees in front of her husband. The naked lady tried to get up and her father tried to zip up his pants, "No," her mother laughed and pointed the gun at them. "Don't stop on my account! You two have been doing this for years and don't think you're the only one, because he swaps you bitches out every other week." She pointed the gun directly toward the lady and gestured downward with the gun, "Get back on your knees and put it back in your mouth."

The lady looked up at her father scared! Her father looked down at her as if to say, "You better suck it!" She inserted his now limp manhood in her mouth, just holding it there. Her mother cocked the gun, and the lady commenced to doing it the way she was before her mother entered the room.
"Babbbbby, I-," her father tried to speak.

"Don't say shit! Let's just enjoy the moment," her mother chuckled

86

"I have watched you beat, belittle, drug and manipulate your wife for years, I stayed quiet and waited. You were making sure she stayed on her meds, so I really didn't have a choice, but I knew one day you would slip up and forget to refill a prescription….You self-serving asshole! And voila, here I am… your worst fucking nightmare… the bitch that don't give a fuck."

She then placed the gun to the woman's cheek while his penis was still between them. Doll turned her head away as she heard a loud bang, and the screams of her father. She then heard another bang! Her mother was lying on the floor, the woman was lying on the floor, and her father was screaming on the floor, holding himself between his legs. She dropped to floor, sobbing, not understanding what just happened. All she knew was her mother was not moving.

The years after that, her father became cruel and bitter regarding her and the world. He had to have surgery on his genitals, and he was never the same. He started giving Doll her mother's medicine, thinking

87

she was going to grow up with the same mental illness as her. He took it upon himself to play doctor, thinking the incident would scar her for life. Her father also had ill fillings concerning her, because she didn't intervene that night. He didn't realize that no matter what, because of his actions, that night was bound to happen. By giving her the pills, if she wasn't crazy before, those pills made her crazy now.

Once Doll came back to the present, Shawna was on top of the girl like video hoes on rappers. Doll laughed at the memory; she always had her back and Doll tutored her as well as had her back too. Her father hated Shawna, said she was a bad seed. He would always say, "That little bitch is going to be a straight up hoe. You need to stay away from that girl, besides she has a lot of jealousy towards your crazy ass."

She didn't see it. Shit… Shawna was always pointing out the things she did wrong, so how was she jealous?

If anything, she was just trying to be real with her to make sure she survived in this corrupt world.

Doll admits that she believed in love, getting a good education, being able to take care of herself, and having a relationship with GOD. However, she wasn't totally naive about the down side of things. On occasion, she did sense some tension from Shawna directed to her, more so this past week. A couple of times she caught her with hate in her eyes as she looked at her. She didn't know what that was about, but as soon as this was over, she was going to see what was up. There was no way in hell she could still feel some type of way about the ATL thing, if anything Doll should be still pissed.

Back in the bedroom

Envy slowly slid down on his dick. She inhaled and gasped, as it filled her insides up. She moaned, as she rotated her hips. She intended to take it slow, but she couldn't contain herself, so she went wild. *"Damn, my baby working it,"* he thought. His mind was so fucked up that he didn't grasp what had happened minutes ago. All he knew, he was dreaming about fucking his woman and now he was in some hot pussy. He grabbed her waist, without opening his eyes. Moving to her rhythm, he moaned, "OOOOOOOOH, Doll Baby, this is your dick!" he said as he encouraged her to keep riding it like stallion, as he smacked her ass.

What the fuck? This nigga *had the nerve to call her that bitch's name. How dare he even think her pussy could be this fucking good?* "Who the fuck is Doll Baby? My name is Envy."

His eyes popped open and he threw her off him. "What the fuck? Get the fuck out!" He didn't want to say anything else to her; he was disgusted with himself.

90

He went on a rampage and threw everyone out. He knew it wasn't her fault, so he would try to find her later to apologize. Shit! What was he going to do? Damn! He didn't even know how the hell the shit happened. Everything was fuzzy; he tried hard to think of how the hell she got into his bedroom. Still feeling sick, he laid back down; his mind wasn't ready for the guilt trip he was about to do to himself.

Envy was mad as hell! She didn't get her nut off and plus that nigga called her that bitch's name! Even with a drugged up nigga, that uppity bitch still wins. *"How in hell is that possible,"* she thought as she drove back to her hotel. No matter what she did, this bitch came up on top. Shit, the reason Doll had so much bad luck with men was, because Envy always seduced them. If that didn't work she told them about her mental illness.

The reason the whole school knew her mom was crazy and killed herself was because of her. She loved Doll. At first, she was her best friend, but Envy started to feel some type of way about all the good things that started happening to Doll. When Doll just upped and left the strip club after two weeks and went to Spelman, Envy was a little pissed, hoping that she didn't make it. Envy wanted money now, not later, after four years of school. Doll was no longer her pet project, she came into her own, and she was getting everything Envy wanted for herself.

"It's all good though…. When it's all over and done, I'm going to get the last laugh," she smiled to herself, as she waited for the elevator to let her off her floor. Shit, I'm about to rock her world either way it go. It doesn't matter that I drugged his ass or he threw me off of him. I still had some of his dick, and it was good. Now it was time to get Doll's ass out of the way. She let out a little laugh as she dialed Doll's number. The resentment in her wouldn't let her tell the truth.

It was about 6 in the morning when Doll got the call. She put the phone to her ear; she just knew it was going to be good news.

"What's up? Baby Doll… Just to let you know, he's still a dog, and I fucked him."

"YOU FUCKED HIM? That wasn't the fucking plan Shawna!" Doll said jumping to her feet.

"Don't get a fucking attitude with me cause your fairytale man turned out to be a dog like the rest of these niggas! I mean, you didn't have me do this to see if he would ALMOST cheat! You wanted to see if he WOULD cheat, so I'm not going to let you make me look like the bad guy! I did you a favor! You should be grateful! I don't fuck for free! Anyways, I'm about to get some beauty sleep. I'll call you tomorrow. I want to hear all about how you tore into his ass and kicked him to the curb." Envy put the receiver down with a devious smile on her face. Now, it was time to get back at Don; plus, if her plan was to work, she needed to see him again. How dare that motherfucker turn her down?

As Shawna put the receiver down, she clicked on her CD player and turned on Trina's *The Baddest Chick*.

Dancing around her luxury hotel suite, her mind was dancing around her plan to steal Mr. Football from Doll, but first she had to get Mr. Football to see her again. A devious smile crept on her face as her plan came into play. The knock at the door interrupted the phone call she had to make. The hotel was already up for two weeks, so they couldn't be coming to escort her out. Not bothering to put on a robe or look through the peephole, she sashayed to the door in her underwear to the beat of her theme song. She grabbed the handle and swung the door open with an attitude, she didn't have time to react as the blow came without warning.

Body flying backward, Shawna hit the coffee table hard. She struggled to get up as she heard the door to the suite slam shut. He turned the music up a tad bit, to muffle out the sounds of revenge he was about to get on this bitch. With no mercy, he yanked her up by her 500 dollar sew-in that he knew he paid for. Shawna's eyes widened with frightening surprise as he grabbed her by the throat, "Where the fuck is my money, Envy?" Jah spat the question in her face.

94

Fresh out, the only thing that was on Jah's mind was Envy. She was the only person on his mind, since she didn't show up to give his sister La La his stash money. He knew something was up. All of a sudden the phone was disconnected and she got ghost real quick. His plan was to get his money, then kill her. However, now seeing her submissive, in a black all lace thong and panty set, his manhood had a different plan. It wouldn't hurt if he played with her devious ass a little while longer.

To him, Envy was an irresistible, poisonous, and exotic creature he had to have. When he met her stripping at Black Cherries, he knew he had to have her. Her body was chocolate and thick; his mouth watered thinking about it. He had to take a minute and fuck her with his eyes. No sex for six months, Jah was caught up in a moment of weakness.
Like the seductress she was, Shawna saw that moment of weakness. She grabbed one of his hands from around her throat. He let her guide his hand away, but he tightened up his grip around her neck with the other.

Slowly, she glided his hand down her body, not even breaking their intense eye contact. She showed no fear, although her heart was beating like the bass from a hard hip hop beat. She moved his hand between her thighs. Moving her thong to one side, Jah instantly caressed her wetness.

His thoughts and body were running on impulses as he moved his fingers in and out of her wetness. She moaned as he rotated his thumb on her clit. He was inflamed…. She knew it, he knew it, and his manhood knew it too. They both knew the affect she had on him, but what he didn't know was the affect he had on her. Jah stopped suddenly; Shawna stopped breathing. Did she fail to take his mind away from the money? Has she lost her touch on the art of seduction, the art of whoredom? She was just about to curse Donovan out in her head for the start of her losing streak. Jah held her gaze; he read the uncertainty in her eyes. Then, a flickering of something imitating regret, revealed itself in Envy's eyes.

The thought of his money didn't leave his mind. It fueled the lustful fire into a fury of vengeful thirst. Her body was captivating, but her surrendering fear was enchanting. The intense stare down was abruptly interrupted by the sinister smirk on Jah's face. Shawna felt his grip around her throat get tighter as he lifted her body up in the air and rammed her body into the wall. Damn… she did lose her touch. She chastised herself. It was futile to kick or scream; there was no telling who Jah had connections with. Jah roughly snatched her panties off of her. The fabric of the lace, forcefully being ripped and snatched upwards, against her womanhood, made her wince, a tear slipped from her eyes. He shoved her panties in her mouth, "I have never seen this side of you before," he laughed in her face as he found the tear oddly out of place. "It's damn right interesting," he teased, as he bit her bottom lip until blood seeped out. He yanked her head down, wrapped her hair around his fist three times, and dragged her by her hair, across the room, and to the bed.

This time, she kicked and tried to get away from the pain, "You wicked, wicked girl…. Where is my money?" he questioned her again, as he dragged and yanked her to the bar area. She knew not to answer him until she could tell him where his money was. Crying for her life was not an option he would have pity on. She watched as he opened a bottle of Ciroc and took a couple of sips out the bottle before he shattered it on the floor. He repeatedly did it to every bottle and glass in the bar, while still tightly gripping her hair. Her having to pay for the damage was the least of her troubles as Jah dragged her through the burning liquid and shattered glass… ass first.

Jah and Envy

Jah picked Envy up and put her body in the bath water he just prepared in the hotel's Jacuzzi tub. He moved Envy and her things to his hotel suite, while the hotel staff cleaned up hers. He watched her not saying a word as she mentally excessed her situation. Jah was a man of few words to him his actions spoke volumes, and the events that happened just an hour ago was as loud as he could get without killing her. He had to look at the bigger picture he wanted her alive for now so she could lead him to Doll.

Envy knew for the time being she will have to come up with a plan to keep Jah at bay! She would have to recruit China and Tora to execute it.

They were born and raised in Nap, they would know the ends and outs to at least the middlemen in Nap. Having the middlemen would lead them to the Elite. "Tell me something! Where Yo Boss at?" will be name of the game, after she twisted these fools' money around her finger.

Envy had two plans; the first plan was to get Donovan to see her again. She refuses to ever let Doll win one over on her. She knew she would have to play dirty to get him to see her. Her plan was to have China hint to Chad that Don raped and put his hand on Envy. China planted it in Chad's ear that she might settle for a price instead of going to the press or the authorities. The last thing Don needed was negative publicity after the pregnancy fiasco.

Next Day

Don couldn't figure out why he couldn't reach Doll, he tried her cell phone, no answer he went to her crib no answer. He was going out of his mind, not knowing, until he heard his messages on his house phone.

"You trifling ass Negro. How dare you fuck somebody in your bed and what soon was supposed to be our bed. I left something for you in the kitchen, after you see

it. You will know why THE WEDDING IS OFF! I DON'T
WANT TO SEE YOUR FUCKING FACE!"

Don ran to the kitchen after he heard Doll's message.
It was two DVD's and her engagement ring lying on the
kitchen table. He was trying to figure out when she
had time to do that. She even gave back her house key.
Damn, his rapid thinking was being interrupted by his
cell phone ringing.

"Don, man what the fuck you do to that girl that
night. Her girl China telling me you gave the girl a
black eye and something about you dragging her through
glass, because she wouldn't fuck you. What the fuck is
going on with you, man?" Chad asked.
"I didn't do shit to that girl. I was up stairs out of
it and here this chick is riding my dick and I threw
the bitch off me. Then I threw her out and yall asses
too. Other than that I didn't touch her. Her shit
seemed fine when I kicked her ass out, didn't she seem
fine to you when you left?"

"Yeah, but, I don't know we were all fucked up, that shit was a blur. Well, you need to talk to that bitch because she's talking about going to the Press with that story. They just sent me the pictures of her via picture messages that chick's ass, lips and eye is fucked up dude. You of all people don't need this shit, you just signed a million dollar endorsement and it has a moral clause in it. Do you understand how just the accusation that a famous football player raped and beat up a female, can become a circus. It doesn't matter if you did it or not. Just the thought of someone thinking you did it, is enough to ruin your whole career. Let's not forget about, Doll, on top of that the bitch got pictures, that's proof dude."

"Rape, I didn't rape that bitch and I didn't put my hands on her." Don couldn't believe his ears how can one night out with the boys result in this.

"You need to talk to that broad, and soon. You need to invite her over and see where her head is. Before she file chargers you need to see if you can pay her

103

some hush money. Don't do it over the phone, you never know who's listening." Chad said hanging up the phone.

Chad grinned at China, who was down on her knees servicing him like no other. "Baby, you sure your girl is going to drop this BS, if my boy talks to her face to face right?" he asked through the sounds of pleasurable slurps and slobs.

"I don't know baby, China said between licks, she's really hurt behind it, plus she has medical bills and she's missing work. Envy has always been a good girl; I don't know what type of mental or emotional damage has been done to my girl. She can be a little too trusting at times." China repeated the whole script as she was told to do. She knew one thing Envy better not fuck up her and Tora's money trains. They had a plan of their own to execute.

***

Don hung up the phone, furiously, this shit cannot be happening he said as grabbed the tapes. The first one was of him lying on the bed and Envy taking off her clothes in front of him. He knew he wasn't conscious but to someone that wasn't there it looked like he was watching her every move. Envy took his draws off and he saw how he lifted his ass up to accommodate her. He shook his head at himself, shit he didn't remember none of that shit. He watched it until he threw her off him, after that he remembered what happened. He popped in the other one bracing himself for what other actions he might have did that night.

Just to think of Doll watching this shit it, it had to break her state of mind. If it broke her that means, she was off her Meds. He had to find out where his woman was, he had to explain himself. Shit what woman would believe him over her own eyes. Especially since, he was known for cheating. As he watched the view of the bar, he saw where he left to go get Envy some wine.

Envy reached in her purse, grabbed a bottle, and dropped some type of white shit into his glass. She grabbed three glasses first and walked out, then that

105

is when he saw himself come back with the wine as she was getting the two remaining glasses. "THIS BITCH! Who the fuck is this bitch?" He called Doll's phone and to his surprise, she answered.

"What?" she said drunkenly

"Doll Baby, how could you be mad at me and you saw the tape? You know what went down on that tape."

"I couldn't watch the damn tape Donovan, I didn't need too. She said sniffling.

"Then how do you know what happened?"

"Look Shawna, Envy whatever is my best friend and she told me she fucked you."

"What-

"Look I couldn't trust you, I wanted to but it's a good thing I didn't. Envy said she would flirt with you in a comfortable environment to see if you would take the bait and cheat on me again. AND YOU DID!" She hung up the phone.

He was at awe at the conniving plan, but how could he blame her, he had hurt her so much. Since she won't look at the tapes, he had to get Envy to tell on herself. Plus he wanted to squash this rape shit. He called Chad to get Envy's number; he had a plan of his own. He knew it was going to take him a couple of days to get everything just right. He *sent a text messaging stating to meet him at his place tomorrow.*

The Underground Playground

The atmosphere dominated the mood of the parking garage; one lone car was sensually placed in the domain of what was to be the grand opening of The Underground Playground, the beginning of a sexually escapade all centered on an expensive man toy.

Envy wanted the local ballers to be their first tryout, which is where China and Tara came in. The two money starving divas were natives of Indianapolis and she was pretty sure they knew who could afford to play in the Underground playground. The key to The U.P. was going to be a text message sent to your phone,

The men all arrived, Jah watched as several street hustlers ventured in, he looked down at his Armani suit and laughed, he was too overdressed for this riff raff. Baggy jeans, White T's, Timberlines or Gym Shoes and over exaggerated Bling. Some had sense enough to wear button downs and some had a little style about them. He looked on as he watched them pull out knots of money, as they went to the bar to purchase drinks. "Well at least these nigga's got money." He thought to himself. He shook his head, but once he took over - depending on the success- he was going to have to upgrade on the Clientele. These were the type to run their mouths about what went on behind closed doors. They were the type to want to brag on the experience. Nothing is wrong with the word of mouth on the low, but these were the ones who would have a round table discussion on this event. It was a good thing that he came up with the idea to switch up on locations and make it invite only. Because, this could go wrong before he could get his money back from Envy. One thing for sure he was going to have to involve his own team, a team of people who would bring in their own touches and their own Elite Clientele to the table.

He had to give it to Envy this idea of hers was not surprisingly ingenious, of course because it's a way for her to save her ass and get some money also. By the looks of it, this would seem to be a very lucrative business idea.

The moment the water sprayed from the three sprinklers "I love them strippers by 2Chainz" came through the speakers, the strobe lights flashed off and on, illuminating the three girls on top of the car. All three girls were dressed in white cut off wife beaters, white cotton bootie shorts with gold bikinis underneath.

"It was okay! Jah said nonchalantly,

Doll

Doll had been off her meds for at least two days; the amount of X pills that Envy left behind was enough to take her mind to a different place. She didn't know how she made it to his house in one piece, but she did. She was running off true anger, she was on the verge of insanity. She couldn't remember how she got the fish guts but she made sure she put it to good use. Doll saw a stash of weed, she never rolled a blunt in her life but you had better believe she made it smoke able. She looked around for something to drink she didn't want to drink just anything she wanted to drink his expensive shit. She grabbed a bottle of Van Gogh; she knew that Gin was damn near 500 a bottle.

Doll wanted to hear DMX, the darkness that overtook her needed theme music and X was the choice for the soundtrack. She inflicted havoc on Don's house, and she wasn't done yet. She grew madder by the minute when it appeared he hadn't been home in a while. She couldn't believe this shit, he asked her to marry him, he cheated again and now he wants to disappear.

Her father voice invaded her mind; she did everything to get him out. She couldn't listen to him; he was the reason why, she was like she was. He made her take her mother's medication for her schizophrenia and the Ambien. To this day she has no idea why he made her take it. If she would have asked she would have known her father was making her take it out of guilt, in the hopes she wouldn't remember what was going on in her life before her mother. For several nights Doll had nightmares and her father just wanted her to shut up. He wanted her to disappear when she was in the house, so he started medicating her.

She didn't start hearing voices and doing crazy shit until after that. Throwing bottles and cursing the voice out only cease it momentarily. She wished she could hear her mother's voice instead. Her father never liked her best friend and he seemed to never have liked his own daughter either, so why would she believe him when he said Envy was no good.

Not once did Doll think of Envy and her part in the scheme of things. To Doll, Envy was the closest thing she had to family, she knew her past but she never once threw it in her face. Envy was always looking out for her with the girls at school to schooling her on her cheating ass men. She taught her how to dress well she at least tried to but Doll couldn't see herself in the clothes Envy wore. She couldn't see herself hanging out with the people she hung out with or doing the things she did. Doll thought it was because she was inadequate to Envy but in reality, she just had more self-respect than Envy did. A car driving up stopped her reminiscing and she looked out the window

***

Envy was smiling from ear to ear as she stepped out of the car with Donovan. *Ms. Goody Goody gave up her man with her dumb ass. Shit fuck that she gave up a life of luxury without getting hard evidence that he actually did cheat. MMMph, always looking down on my clothes and shit, as if she were better than I was. Went off to college and got uppity and shit like she didn't come from where I'm from. Let me quit I'm ruining this victorious moment;* she smiled to herself as she hummed The Baddest Bitch by Trina.

Donovan knew he would have to hold all he knew and felt about this bitch in. He had the camera already set up in the basement, this bitch was going to get him his girl back and the rape charges won't even come to fruition after this.

He opened the door and it smelt a little funky, but he thought that maybe it was the garbage he hasn't been home since yesterday. He didn't cut on any lights he went directly to his basement, made for entertaining.

***

After she saw them pull up, Doll ran to the basement to hide in the wine cellar. She had something for both of their asses. She reasoned with herself into believing that maybe Envy came over there to give him a piece of her mind. She'd wait until Envy left to finish Don off, but her father was in her mind telling her to kill them both and then do herself. She thought he was wrong until she heard Envy say

"So you found out hunch. Weak bitch, I mean we used to be friends and shit before she went off to college. She always thought she was too good for hood shit, on the low always trying to call me out. She wasn't no true friend, I put up with the bitch because she used to let me control her life. And evidently she still will." she laughed.

"Damn so you just played a brother just because. Right?"

"Man that shit wasn't my idea. The only reason I agreed to it was because I felt bad for you. I mean here you are giving this girl the world and your last name. And she don't even trust you, on top of that she do some scandalous shit like this. Shiiit, I knew I deserved everything she was trying to give up. And once I saw your picture, I wanted you for myself. I figured I could treat you better than she can. She gulped down her fifth drink and the pills were kicking in.

"See this is what I don't get man, I can't remember shit but bringing yall to the house, I remember the living room incident but then after that it's blank. Now, I remember kicking you out and everybody else. But, shit that is it. So since we keeping it real and shit, tell me what went down that night."

"Okay, don't get mad but I put two x pills in your drink. Look, I did it for your own good; you weren't even trying to rub up against a bitch. You were being faithful to the wrong bitch. And I knew if we didn't do anything that she would marry someone she didn't deserve."

"WOW-

A crash and Doll coming towards Envy with fury in her eyes stopped his sentence. "Baby, What- He couldn't get it out. Envy reacted too late her back was to Doll, she wrapped an extension cord around Envy's neck. She tried to struggle as she kicked and clawed as Doll pulled her to the middle of the floor.

Doll had one hand on the nine and the other wrapped around the cord that was strangling Envy, her strength had doubled but she didn't realize it. Don did, he knew she was off her meds, so he couldn't just go to her and pull her off Envy. Besides he rather thought the bitch deserved it. Envy maliciously tried to destroy their lives all because she envied the way life had turned out for Doll. But, what she didn't know was Doll suffered from a real mental illness that was triggered by depression. Her mind wasn't rational the goody goody that Envy once knew was gone and now this was her alter ego. Her mind was engulfed with voices and all of them chanted "Kill Her!"

Doll wouldn't let go Oh, she wouldn't let go until she breathed her last breath. "YOU JEALOUS ASS HO, "she yelled! As she stopped pulling her by her neck with cord and she started beating her with the butt of the gun.

Her father was laughing, hysterically now, "Told you, you were crazy. I told you, you're just like your mother. You should have gotten rid of the bitch a long time ago. You about to go to jail, you about to go to jaillll." Her father sung.

"SHUT THE FUCK UP, she yelled as she waved the gun in the direction that the voice was coming at. She was too busy trying to get a pin on her father's voice to shoot him for the last time. She let go of the cord.

At first not able to catch her breath Envy quickly knocked the gun out of her hand it flew across the floor, both women went for it, fighting each other along the way. Wasn't shit Don could do, he knew the doctors said not to confront her when she was like this. If he did, he knew she would more likely harm herself and him. It was better this bitch than him. What was he supposed to do hold her at gunpoint and tell her to get those crazy motherfuckers out her head? Doll reached the gun first and cocked it; she pointed it dead at Envy.

"Baby, put that shit down. She's not worth it. It's one thing to beat the fuck out of her but kill her hell no. I can't let you go to jail over some scandalous ass HO." He slowly walked in her direction out of the aim of the gun.

Doll trembled with hate.

Envy trembled with fear. If she would have known this bitch was really crazy she would have never tried some shit like this. Here she was envying her life, all the things Doll accomplished, and she was dealing with some Girl Interrupted, shit. She was about to die and Why? Because she wanted the life Doll had...

Doll had tears coming down her face in anger, trembling with hate

Envy had tears coming down her face in fear, trembling with regrets.

Don slowly crept closer; Doll's father's voice crept even closer and closer

"Shoot the Bitch! Shoot the Bitch! Pop goes the mother fucking weasel!"

"Baby, put it down."

"Shoot the Bitch; Shoot the Bitch, ha ha. Shoot her!" I'll never say you're like your mother again if you just shoot the bitch. Let me see if you got it in you." Don was almost there.

Her father was already there; his voice was coming from where Envy was standing.

"YOU STUPID BITCH, YOU CAN'T DO IT CAN YOU. I ALMOST HAD RESPECT FOR YOU. YOU ARE JUST LIKE YOUR MOTHER! WEAK, YOU LET EVERYBODY RUN OVER YOU. YOU THINK THIS HATING ASS BITCH WILL LET YOU GET AWAY WITH THIS SHIT. SHE'S NOT, SHE HAS BALLS, JUST KILL YOURSELF-"I SAID JUST SHUT THE FUCK UP, she screamed as she shot in the direction of her father's voice. Her shot was off as the figure behind her came out of the shadows; the bullet hit the screen of the T.V.

As Jah pushed Doll to the side he charged at Don quickly before anyone knew what was transpiring, he knocked him over the head with the butt of his gun. Don fell face first onto the glass table, he was out cold.

Jah pointed his gun at Doll, Envy sighed in relief as if Jah came to her rescue. She never once questioned why he was there, her mind was occupied on the fact that this bitch was about to kill her. Something she never knew Doll had the balls to do.

"Alright, Ladies and I use that term loosely, this catfight is now over. Both of you out to the backyard," he said waving his gun at them both.

Doll recognized him from somewhere but at the moment the murder that was still on her mind stopped her mental from forming that visual. He lead them to the car, Envy was a little at ease then Doll was. Of course Jah wouldn't do anything to her, shit she was his business partner over the weeks that she had come up with the business plan, and she has paid him back tenfold. The girls and Envy were making him a great deal of money with The Underground Playgrounds. He also was making bigger moves with his investment banking due to the elite clientele they were entertaining during their events.

Jah watched Doll with intensity, a longing; she was the more mature version of his dead girlfriend Jazzy. He wanted to get to the bottom of what happened that

119

night. He knew because he couldn't reach the hit men

in time was the reason that her life was taken.

However, it didn't take away from the fact that, it

was because of these two that it went down, he thought

they had Jazzy caught up in some shit she didn't want

to be in.

"Drive," he told Envy! He threw Doll into the

passenger seat as he sat in the back with his gun

strategically pointed at them both.

Envy was smiling inside as she mugged Doll out of the

corner of her eye. In her head she thought Doll must

be sitting over there scared shitless just like she

had her in that damn basement. To her astonishment

Doll was looking at her head on, with murder still in

her eyes. Envy swallowed hard and converted her eyes

back on the road as Jah gave directions.

Jah was amused, Doll wasn't a punk, regardless of who

she thought he was, rather or not if he were in

cahoots with Envy or not. She still showed her

disguise for Envy. Her eyes still had that killer look

in them ready for any opportunity to yank her

esophagus out of her throat. He saw the fear in Envy's eyes; she wasn't as tough as she thought she was. He heard the shit she was throwing out there when she was downing Doll, playing her as a weak bitch. He realized Doll was nothing like that which made him want her more. He wanted her but nothing would ever make him forget what she had done to his girlfriend.

"Pull over here," he navigates Envy on the road to the deserted playground as if she were in on whatever he had planned. In Envy's head she was his conspirator, she knew she made him too much money for him to even harm one hair on her head. Besides why would he come to her rescue just to kill her?

Jah had this place set up for this reason alone, "Grab her," Jah told Envy as he got out the car with his gun pointed at both of them. Gladly to do his bidding she grabbed hold of Doll. Doll looked at Envy's hand as she tried to grab her arm, "You can fucking touch me if you want, she spat at her as she bumped past her to walk on her own.

Envy swallowed hard but quickly gained her composure in her moment of uncertainty. Doll was more woman than she thought and the way she acted at the house she didn't know if the bitch would attack her and bite her fucking ear off. Regardless of the gun on her Envy had a feeling it wasn't over between them. But hopefully Jah wouldn't let anything happen to her.

As they entered both women were grabbed by Jah's henchmen and roughly handcuffed to the two stripper poles that were placed in the middle of the warehouse. "What the fuck is this Jah?" Envy hollered out in pain.

Jah waved his index finger in the no-no fashion as he spoke calmly, "I don't need you to speak. I don't want you to speak. What you two are going to do now is listen to this story and answer some questions." Jah grabbed a chair and lit up his Newport. His henchmen stood on command with their guns pointed both at Envy and Doll. "You know what, why prolong it?" He said dumping his ashes onto the ground.

"I'll just ask the questions, but first my men want to have a little fun. The henchmen moved in closer to the girls, grinning and massaging their growing man hoods inside of their pants.

Jah gave the man closest to Doll a head nod. Doll watched the interaction and looked in the direction of the man moving toward her. She was ready to bite, kick; head butt any one of those, Wrestlemania looking mother fuckers. Doll had a feeling she was about to be raped and God only knows what else so she was going to give them hell.

The henchman approached Doll with caution as he bent her over so her ass protruded up in the air, the short pleated black skirt she had on risen to show her red thong, the henchmen couldn't resist he bent down bit her on the ass before he slid the barrel of the gun through the strings. He played there for a while rubbing the steel between her flesh and the string of her thong, then with a sudden motion he used the gun to rip the thong from her body.

"Motherfucker, Doll side kicked his ass. Somebody should have yelled timber when his big ass hit the floor; her kick was just that powerful. He jumped up ready to pounce, "Gab, Jah said silenced his actions by calling his name. Gab stopped in his tracks, un-cuffed Doll, "Get your ass on the floor, Bruce Lee!" he told her waving his gun toward the floor. Doll positioned herself down on the floor as she was told, but still had the look of defiance on her face. She was ready to buck at any minute.

"Spread your legs," he told her.

She slightly opened them, "Naw wider!" he told her as he kicked her legs open to the degree in which they wanted them. Doll breathed a sigh of relief when Gab didn't come toward her. He had moved on to Envy now un-cuffing her from the pole, then re-cuffing her hands together. Gab then stepped back into his position and waited for Jah to continue.

"Envy, I want to see your linguistics skills." Jah informed her. Envy got down on her knees in front of Doll. It's not like she hasn't went down on a female before for money so shit she'll do it again if it spared her life. As she was about to put her mouth on Doll she noticed the tampon string hanging out. "Shitting me, she said jumping up; the men quickly pointed their guns at Envy ready to fire if needed.

"What's the problem? Jah asked

"This bitch is on her period!" Envy said in disgust folding her arms in the process.
The room erupted with laughter.

Jah laughed also, but it was a sadistic laugh, "I don't give a fuck if shit was coming out of her pussy. Down girl!" he told her, as he gave his men a head nod. All the men came closer with their weapons drawn and fingers on their triggers. "Better a bloody mouth than a bloody body. Wouldn't you say, Shawna?"

The laughter continued as Envy made her way down to Doll's bloody vagina. Doll was in disgust herself even with the hatred she had for Envy she couldn't fathom making someone do that blood or not. She especially was not down for Envy eating her out period; she never let her before in her stripper days so you know she wasn't happy with it now. She just better hope she doesn't snap her neck while she was down there.

"Go ahead you're a naughty girl pull it out with your teeth. " Jah laughed
Envy's face was so close she could see the blood clot in the enter way to Doll's vagina. She tasted the fast arrival of vile in her mouth, it was one thing she could say at least Doll didn't have a repugnant smell to her. She held out her tongue closed her eyes and flicked her tongue on Doll's clit.

"I've witnessed you eat pussy before Envy so I know you can do better than that!" Jah told her. Jah gave a nod and two of the henchmen took a step closer and cocked their guns and placed the barrel to her head. Envy could feel the cold steel up pressed against her head. She had no choice but to close her eyes and give Doll the best tongue lashing she could muster.

Lying there Doll didn't feel a thing she couldn't, she was numb. She focused on the gunmen and trying to determine her fate in all of this. There was no way this could be about her maybe Envy got her into some shit again. Somewhere in the back of her mind she was wondering where she has met Jah before on where she had come across his face.

Doll eyed the gunmen and it seemed they were getting a kick out of this performance the proof was in their growing erections.

"Doll, grab her head and fuck her face! I want to see you enjoy it. I want to hear you moan. I want to hear you cum. I want to see you squirt all over her face and in her mouth!" Jah was directing the scene into the show he wanted to see. He was toying with them now, but he was also contemplating on what he really wanted to do with Doll. Did he want to make her take Jazzy's place or did he just want her dead? He wanted to know what part Envy played in it, plus she was just a trifling ass individual so he was doing this to punish her. One thing he needed to know was the whole truth about what happened in that hotel room.

He got up out of his chair as Doll grabbed Envy's face; she thrust her pussy into it. Now, she was involuntarily feeling something she experienced a powerful orgasm coming. Jah watched intensely as he looked at his dead girlfriend's twin beautiful face in mid orgasm. Standing over them he notice the look and knew that at that moment she was about to come, he yanked Envy's head back so he could witness Doll's pussy squirt.

A loud moan escaped Doll's mouth as she released and sure enough she squirted, embarrassed for her and Envy, she laid there a shamed of herself.
Jah pulled Envy up to Doll's mouth and forced their mouths together, "Taste yourself, I want to see tongue! "He warned them. Doll tasted her nectar as well as her blood on Envy's tongue as their tongues danced around each other loathing every step to the dance they were dancing. He pulled them apart, both women were gagging and trying to wipe the evidence of what they had done out of their mouths.

"Now, let's see who is the baddest bitch between you two? I am going to ask some questions and all I want is truthful answers, the most ruthless will win.

Have you ever fucked over a friend and she lost her life because of you? "Jah eyed Doll Envy laughed because she knew she had Doll beat hands down. She knew what story she was going to tell to show that Doll was not the ruthless one. Despite the episode at Don's house Envy felt that nobody held a candle to her when it came to being out for self by any means necessary.

Doll had a look of sorrow in her eyes as Jazzy came into mind. "Doll you look like you have a story to tell, proceed." Jah told her.

"I, Doll started and paused to gather herself, I let the wrong influence get around my best friend and she ended up dead because of it." Doll meekly finished

"This bitch didn't have shit to do with that. You want to hear ruthless, I will tell you ruthless. Her soft ass didn't have the balls to go make some money but her dumb ass roommate did. Anyways, I left her gullible country ass friend in a room to get raped. I knew she wasn't going for anyone fucking her, but they wanted to and those College boys were paying extra. Captain Save A Ho over there, she said pointing to Doll. Decides she wants to intervene and rescue her. I mean sit the stupid bitch was so gung ho on wanting to strip; she should have known what came with it. So long story short I had to come to the rescue had to shoot a nigga and then we robbed them. I kept the money and got of dodge, while her and her best friend stayed to do their whole College thing. They found the other girl and killed her thinking she could lead them to the money, I guess. Who knows and who gives a fuck?" Envy boasted to Jah. Envy knew she lied about the shooting the dude but she knew Doll mind was occupied with thoughts of her so called best friend. Envy did feel some type of way about that, regardless of what she put Doll through.

Jah kept calm as he witness angry tears running down Doll's face. Doll didn't talk Jazzy into anything, and it wasn't a case of mistaken identity. Jazzy might not have been the girl who killed his cousin, but she was involved. He can tell Doll blamed herself for her death, because of her association with Envy's malicious ass.

Jah slowly unbuttoned his shirt to reveal the face he had tattooed on his heart. Doll and Envy were both confused of the tattoo, it looked exactly like

Doll. Jah walked closer to Doll, as he came closer the writing of the name bewildered her for a second.

"Bone?" She asked, Envy set there confused while Jah had his back to her, she just knew she was in the clear so she relaxed and waited for the gunshots to be penetrated into Doll's body. Better Doll than her!

"Jazzy's Jah?" She asked, pictures of him now vividly flashing through her head.

Jah nodded towards Doll and then nodded again in the other direction, Gab quickly swooped up Doll, with her fighting every step of the way. Envy was hysterically laughing, "Ah ha Bitch! See it pays to have friends in low places Ms. Goody Goody! You ain't never had a friend like -." Envy was too busy teasing Doll , that she didn't feel Jah come up behind her. Jah grabbing Envy's head by her mouth and the back of her skull, twisting with a sudden violent jerk, breaking her vertebrae! She instantly collapses to the floor.

Gab finally getting Doll outside, "Calm your crazy ass down!" he told her as he threw her in the driver's seat of her own car. She didn't even think twice when she saw the keys in the ignition; she cranked that mother fucker up and sped home.

* * *

"Chop her up, burn her and fertilize her grandmother's garden with her." He told them as he grabbed his cell, "Yo, Roc Vega! What up Big Dog? I need you to go into a business venture with me!

"What do you have in mind, Big Dog" Vega questioned

"Shit, the sweetest business in the world my friend- Pussy!" Jah laughed into the phone.

"You came to the right man, my feline game is just as superior as my cannabis indica game. I know quality pussy and head!" Vega laughed.

"This is what I know! Welcome to The Elite Feline of The Underground Playgrounds! " Jah welcomed him as he lit his cigar.

La La's Story

China/Chocolate Cocaine

China was promised to the Prominent African Dr. for payment of her father's medical bills. China's parents and Dr. Linton knew each other from their home country in Africa. China was born in America; hence, the name China but her last name will be Oniah.

She wanted her father to continue his cancer treatment so when her father signed over his rights to Dr. Johanon Linton, she did not protest. Of course, at the age of 16, she didn't want to be married, she wanted to do what other American teens did. China knows she is being sold like cattle, used as a bartering commodity for medical reasons.

China had craved for a life of luxury before her father became sick their family was on their way to live in the suburbs and owning their own home. Then the devastating blow of Cancer KO'd the breadwinner of the family. China was left with a faded grasp on financial stability, which left hunger. She was blinded by the precious Dr.'s promise to have the ability to cure her father, to care that she had been bought.

So, to the people who were outside looking in, they saw a lucky poverty ghetto stricken the little black girl, get real life rags to riches story. As if she was Willis from A Different Strokes, except her Mr. Drummond was an African Dr. who liked to fuck the mouth of his so called adopted daughter. Whose teeth still after two years and a name change, still managed to nick the flesh of Dr. Linton's penis.

Johanon decided to take matters into his own hands, in Africa he was able to do what he wanted to his wives. To him being an African man in America did not make it any different. He was above American Laws in his household, so if he wanted to adjust his Wife's appearance to enhance his sexual pleasure then so be it. He would give China one more try on her oral skills if it did not surpass his expectations he will go to extreme measures.

China on her knees, orally ready to please her husband, hoping she would please him or he would guide her in the art of fellatio. She went down on his manhood, trying hard to imitate what she had seen in porn movies. She felt as her teeth grazed the skin of his penis, to her surprise he let it pass. The second time was not so forgiving.

"No!" he yanked her up by her hair and harshly threw her towards the chair that was in the middle of the room. Oddly China never paid attention to this new contraption that was now sitting in their bedroom. Frustrated, however, determined to show this young American black girl how NOT to use her teeth.

Now seeing the contraption with its traps and head gear, China's confusion turned into fear. The

138

chair resembled an electric chair for death row inmates. China hurriedly tried to get herself up, a punch to the stomach made her body renege on that option.

China awakened with her body confined to the holdings of the chair, she couldn't even move her head to look around the now pitch black room. She could not feel her body, she could not speak and as China tried to swallow she could not, her mouth was pried open with some kind of metal device.

She was only able to let the tears fall from her eyes for the unknown possibilities of her predicament. She could not only move her limbs, but she also could not feel them either hindering her from even wiggling her fingers or toes.

China was frozen in her own body, her voice, her screams, her cries, were all imprisoned in her body. She knew she wasn't dead her lungs still worked, her eyeballs were still in motion, frantically surveying the room of darkness. She no longer knew if she was still in their bedroom. Fear grew as it clutched at her insides, as the above light was cut on. She squinted at the brightness and let her eyes adjust to the light. She wished she hadn't changed them because standing above her with surgical gloves and dental pliers were Johanon.

Lowering the pliers to her pried opened mouth, "This way," he told her while adjusting the pliers around one of her teeth. "We won't have to worry about you using your teeth."

Darkness blanketed the unknown of her surroundings once again, the coldness of the room was like that of a hospital room, and the humming of some type of machine occupied the air, leaving Chyna to awake to a cold as hell. Her wits were a little foggy, she felt drugged, however, flashes of what happened before her awakening sent her into panic mode. As if that was not enough she had something cold running through her veins, feeling around her body with her hands she felt a cord attached to a needle embedded in her veins.

Finally, her eyes adjusted to the darkness and she realized that there was a glow from the machine that she had seen in hospitals monitoring her heart rate. Her eyes followed the cord up to the steel hanger that held three bags of clear liquid; all three were pumping into her veins.

Panicking she tried to move her legs out of the bed, they did not budge. She frantically tried to reach her legs to see if they were still there. She could only lift her body from the waist up to feel her legs. What the fuck did this nigga do to me? Chyna questioned the powers that be, looking for some type of escape even though she couldn't move, she was thinking about her next move.

She tried to lick her lips and realized she had no top teeth or bottom teeth in the front, a tear slide down her face. This sadistic, selfish motherfucker, she quickly wiped the tears from her eyes. The squeak of the floor was faintly heard over the buzzing of the machine, only when the key entered the lock did she slam her eyes closed. She saw the brightness of the door being opened slide across her closed eyelids.

Footsteps shuffled towards her, falling short by her bedside he fumbled with the cord connected to her veins and the bags of clear liquid. She felt her whole upper body become paralyzed just like her bottom half; she did not dare react or give herself away. It was obvious that whoever this was, that they thought she was still out of it.

Using her ears to listen to his footsteps, he walked across the room to a side door to let someone in, she peeked and that someone was her husband. In her mind she could not think of anything else he could possibly do to her, he now had her the way he wanted her. However she would be mistaken, with surgical gloves both men came towards one with a needle, the other with his hands coming towards her mouth.

Johanon pries her mouth open and puts a mouth prop in it while the other doctor injected her with Lidocaine. Undressing Johanon mounted Chyna's face and entered his penis into her numb opened mouth, first going slow then quickly. Enjoying the sensation of his project, basking in the demonic glow of power that he now possessed over his wife, the pleasure was to no measures.

The other doctor was not to penetrate his wife but he could give her oral pleasure because he was never going to indulge in that American way of life. An un-Americanized African man would never belittle himself to give a woman pleasure. The pain was for the woman. The pleasure was for the man. They brutalized her body, over and over again all night, Johanon semen being dispensed all over her body and the other doctor licking it up was the only indication that they were done.

She refused to cry, the time for crying has relinquished itself somewhere and the growth of fury and revenge had come. In the wee hours of one morning, she found herself in a hospital in another state, in another city. In her belongings were over a thousand dollars, a picture of her fixed teeth and a threatening fuck off letter from her husband.

He deveined her of pride, lied to her, took her innocence and manipulated her body into what he wanted and just threw her away like a sacrificed animal carcass. This was not over, she will make her way back to him and his friend and it was not because she loved him.

Her innocence was presumed dead and her mindset was that of getting money, fuck these sadistic as men. She didn't know shit about Indianapolis, Indiana but, she was about to find her way at the age of 18. Indianapolis could not be worse than Brooklyn, NY.

In China's belongings, she found the name Bone, car keys, a map to the vehicle and an address. She did not know what it meant but she had a good feeling about whoever Bone was.

She arrived at the address, it was a Mansion located far from the hospital she had awakened in, the GPS in the car was already set and she just followed the voice. There was an actually Bellhop at the door in uniform.

"Yes?" he asked

"Bone, she answered

China guesses those were the magic words because he held the door open for her, "Stop at the desk." He informed her. China gladly walked through and onto the desk.

"China."

"Mr. Bone will meet you in the lobby in an hour, so you can get yourself comfortable." The lady at the desk said.

"Thank you," China grabbed the keys and sashayed up the stairs to her suit. Now, that she was here she did not know how to feel. She was presented with this lifestyle already and look how that shit turned out.

La La

It was a warm day; the sunlight blessed the living room and the open kitchen with sun rays. In red boy shorts, white t-shirt, socks and house shoes stood a 5'3 La La with her hair in a ponytail, cooking her husband's favorite dish southern fried smothered chicken with garlic mashed potatoes. As she dunked each piece of the crispy fried chicken into her homemade gravy she couldn't help but take a bite into the chicken breast dripping in gravy.

She giggled to herself as she shook her head at her raging pregnancy hormones, she decides not to be selfish and hopefully by the time she got upstairs with the piece of chicken she was eating, it would still be some left for him.

As she journeyed her way into the living room to the stairs, a strange feeling in her stomach came about, Que! She screamed. Hearing his wife's screams, he bolted downstairs in only his boxers, only to stop in the middle of the staircase. She was standing at the bottom of the stairs with a piece of chicken, smiling as she held her stomach.

"What the hell you screaming for?" he asked her as she came to meet him in the middle of the stairs. She placed his hand on her stomach; he smiled as he felt his child move around for the first time.

"That's my little boy!" she told him as she playfully moved his hand away from her stomach. She bit into the chicken and tried to bypass him on the stairs as if she wasn't coming to give him a bite of chicken.

Que snatched the chicken out of her hand and lifted her off her feet careful not to hurt her or his child. He carried her to their bedroom; he lightly tossed her on the bed and started taking his underwear off. She scooted back on the bed all the while staring at him with love. Oh, you want this don't you? He asked her as he sat the plate on the table and bit into the chicken with one hand, and stroked his hard penis even harder with the other.

"Yeah, I want it!" she told him licking her lips.

"I know you do with your freaky ass. Come get it then!" he told her with a slick grin on his face still eating on the delicious piece of chicken. La La go on her knees crawled to him seductively all the while giving him eye contact. She was face to face with his manhood; Jacques was ready to feel his wife's lips. He leaned his head back anticipating the wetness of her lips; he forgot the chicken was still in his hand. Eyes still closed he felt the piece of chicken being snatched out of his hand and his wife's laughter filled the air. He couldn't help but laugh as he opened his eyes to see his wife devouring the rest of the chicken breast.

"Oh, so you want to play with a nicca? He asked grabbing for her red boy shorts pulling them over her thighs. She playfully struggled and giggled as she ate the piece of chicken that was almost gone. He finally was able to pull them all the way off; he threw them on the floor. He spread her legs; he laid his upper half in between them and licked up her thighs until he reached her yoni. He went in tongue first dipping in and out of her hole, twirling his tongue around her walls. He heard her moan, peeking at her told him what he needed to know, her face showed pure bliss, but she was still holding on to the chicken bone.

He laughed, "Ghetto ass, give me that damn chicken bone." He took the chicken bone and placed it on the nightstand. "Trying to hold on to that chicken like I'm not putting my tongue game down." He watched her laugh and her belly moved at the same time.

He went up to kiss his baby. "Now you got my little girl laughing at me too." He joked

La La stopped laughing but still kept a smile on her face. "I love you, King!" she told him sincerely and the look on her face showed him that her love was unconditional.

"I love you, Queen!" he told her with the same sincerity. He pressed his lips to hers, giving her a deep kiss then trailing kisses back to where he started and, this time, there were no noises of chicken being eating only moans of pleasure between a husband and wife.

Hours later

She was awoken to being probed with a wet tongue, she smiled to herself, and her husband was insatiable. However, something felt unfamiliar, she peered down between her legs and there was a strange face violating her husband's possessions. She didn't panic, she looked to see if anyone else was in the

room or if she could hear any other sounds then this
stupid non-pussy eating motherfucker munching on her.

There was no indication that anyone else was in
the room or in the house, she was not naïve to believe
that he was only on in the house. She knew for sure
they were the only two in the room. The intruder was
too busy to notice that his victim was awake and fully
aware of what was going on. La La tightened her legs
around his neck like a vice grip, she crossed her legs
at the ankles and before he knew it she did a
maneuver, all you heard was the sound of his neck
cracking.

Easing quietly off the bed she grabbed the red
boy shorts her husband took off of her earlier and
slipped them on. She tied her shoe strings together
and hung her shoes over her shoulder by the strings.
She slowly opened the bedroom closest pressed a button
and got her glock no need to load it, it was ready to
go. Stopping at her bedroom door, she listened for

sounds upstairs, satisfied with no one being up there she crept downstairs on her tiptoes. La La knew depending on where the crew was, she was going to have to shoot her way out of the house to safety.

The voices of several men caught her attention, their men gathered on the inside of the porch relaxing as if they did not have a care in the world. Which meant that either her husband was dead or not in the house. Her heart started beating rapidly and her stomach was still as if her child knew that her mother needed silence. She couldn't panic now, she couldn't think of "the what if's" concerning her husband. She needed to get the fuck out of this situation alive to avenge his death or orchestrate his rescue, she was hoping for the latter. It was several doors that lead to the inside porch lucky for her one of them was right next to her stairs. That would bring her right in the back of the intruders, giving her the advantage to kill a couple of them and make her escape to the back of the house.

She studied them for a couple of seconds some were smoking, one was sitting and the other three were facing the one sitting down. None of them had a weapon in their hands, their weapons were either lying on the floor up against the window sill or in their holsters on the side of them. She steadied her body up against the wall; she tiptoed sideways downstairs to the side door.

She put her hand on the nob knowing that she will have to do this fast, and shoot precisely. La La checked to make sure her safety was off the gun; she aimed her gun and twisted the knob slowly, then swiftly opened the door and started shooting. Bullets went into their targets, the first man went down and fell through the window. A piece of glass sliced one of their faces as her bullets entered his chest. The last man landed on top of the man that was sitting on the window sill as her bullet pierced his brain.

She didn't wait to see if the man confined to the floor by the last man she shot was still alive. She really didn't know how much time she had until her backup came or how many others there were. She heard a gun cock as she was running; she glanced back once as she saw a white bald headed man coming around the corner trying to get his fun cocked. Looking back she ran right into a hard muscled body that picked her up, as she felt other people run by her shooting. She fought hard in this unknown person's arms. "Calm down La La!" she heard the person scream. She sighed in relief as she recognized the voice.

"Where's Que?" he asked.

"He wasn't here when I woke up." She told him as the realization of the situation overwhelmed her, tears slid down her eyes. She just might have lost the love of her life. She didn't know how she was going to live without him, but she knew that if she had to, the people responsible was not going to live.

"No, matter what we will find out! But right now we are going to have to get you somewhere safe until you have the baby. After that we can find him together by you working undercover for me at the Underground Playgrounds!" her brother told her.

Tara/Oasis

Tara was a privileged girl, private schooling, expensive cars and shopping sprees. Her lifestyle came with a price, a price where her parents scheduled her every move, they controlled who she hung out with, who she dated, how she dressed and what she was going to do with the rest of her life.

She was spoiled, but she does exactly what her parents tell her to do. She did not want to blemish her father's image in high society. She already slipped up and did just that. So, she made sure she was on her square from then on.

What the fuck is the world coming to, when a girl like me can't buy shit, Tara thought, as she watched the sales lady with pride cut up her credit card. It was as if somebody was making sure she had to accept the job at the Kennedy's. It was something about the way Prof. Kennedy looked at her that didn't sit too well with her.

Damn, her father or should she say step-father was not playing. He couldn't see why she turned down a good job, with good people. She had to give her parents an entirely adequate reason as to why. She had none; it was just something about Mayor Kennedy and Professor Kennedy that she did not like. She always got an eerie feeling when she came in contact with them. She did not like the vibe she would get from Professor Kennedy every time he would pull her to the side.

She knew her reputation as being a spoiled rich chick that fucks her teachers. But, that was only one time, and he wasn't married. You know how things run amuck in high society, rumors behind the privileged are usually embellished with truths, fiction, and pettiness.

One thing about Tara is she usually told the truth; she didn't care who it hurt, she was going to say it like it is. So sitting across from Prof. Kennedy as he gave her glass of soda and ice, she gulped it down, "I do not know about taking this job, sometimes you make me uncomfortable." She slurred grabbing her head.

Tara began to go in and out of consciousness, "Are you okay?" she heard a male voice faintly say

She shook her head, yes, but she knew something was going on with her body. So she felt the need to be in the comfort of her home, "I think I should go home."

"No, you don't look so good. Try to take another sip of your soda. Maybe that will help." He told her with concern in his voice.

Tara started thinking she might have been wrong about Prof. Kennedy's intentions. She had felt that he kept giving her bad grades so that he could be alone with her any chance he could get. His eyes' molested her entire body as soon as she walked into the classroom. She could feel his eyes on her throughout his entire lectures.

Now, he seemed concerned about her like a caring parent. "Maybe, you should lie down," He told her leading her to their guest room. I will call my wife and let her know you are here. I will call your parents and let them know you are ill."

The Professor left Tara alone and then made a couple of phone calls. Tara felt lightheaded and groggy; she laid down on the bed. She only meant to lie there to gather herself, but she soon dozed off. Waking up dazed, she was in an unfamiliar place, trying her best to sit up, she noticed a red glow to the room, giving it a demonic feeling.

She finally adjusted her vision to her surroundings; fear captured her scream in her throat as she saw masked faces encompassing her, and she fainted. When she had awakened, her sore body was being pulled out of her burning house, thrown into a black car with tinted windows and with a blindfold cutting across her face.

She never once was un-blindfolded during the whole trip, she was treated with sympathetic hands, and she could tell a female handled her but a male directed her. Why did she feel safe as of now, with the unknown? However, in danger of people whom she had known from the same circle of her parents. She feared the one whose face she saw running her city; she feared the one's face she saw damn near every day, and probably a gang of people that spoke to her or her parents daily, behind masked and robes. Her mind was still foggy as to why she should fear these people, but she felt it in her soul.

Her secret escape took her as far as a Mansion in Indianapolis, Indiana, where she first met the most beautiful chocolate girl she had seen on the cover of a fashion magazine. They were both instructed to do one thing, and that was to get noticed by Envy and do anything she wanted them to do.

Jah had a reason to keep Tara close to him; she was one of the girls he would keep no matter what. He was told about this group's activities, and he had vowed that he would seek revenge. They had drugged that girl so she couldn't recall what happened to her, that night but when Jah was done with her, she would know why she would be killing her parents' most inner circle and why her parents died. All he needed was his first two girls to hook up with the first person whom he needed to seek his revenge on; he needed to get them closer to Envy, which in term will get him closer to who was responsible for the death of his one love.

After days of following Envy and finding Doll, the plan was already ago, and the more Envy thought she had one up on him, the less she did. Now, that they had already gotten the Underground Playground ago, it was now time for him to take it to the next level.

Tara sat in the meeting room, "Are you ready?" he questioned her. He wasn't even sure he was prepared for the seventeen-year-old to watch what happened to her that night.

The big screen flickered as the scene of a familiar place came into view, the eeriness and the sadistic atmosphere surrounding her and the people in masks were all too similar to the Urban Thriller Ether by Mahogany Bang, which she had just read.

She watched as these masked cloaked figures tied her young body to the wooden bedposts with the coarse gold rope made out of barbwire. Tara automatically ran her fingers across her wrists. The imprint of the marks it left was still visible; she recoiled at the sight as if she could still feel the rope cut into her flesh. She watched as men and women had their way with her young body, poking, stabbing, licking, fucking, burning, whipping were all done to her body, without her being aware of anything. Tara's body was taken in every inconceivable way, with objects that might have given her pleasure and a plethora of pain.

The end of the nightmare left her in a state of hatred, hatred that screamed out obscenities as she tore each black masked cloak wearing motherfucker to pieces with her teeth. The odium was more relevant when she dug her nails into the arms of the chair, as she watched two of the cloaked figures de-robbed and de-masked to reveal themselves as her parents.

Tara slowly lifted her body up from the chair, motion for Jah to give her the video. She broke it in pieces over the garbage can; she walked out of Jah's office with nothing left to be said or how it was going to go down. She was just going to make sure she was ready when it does.

She went back to the hotel suite Bone put her and China in; China was not there, and readily Tara took her clothes off in the middle of the room. She walked over to their bar naked and poured a glass of Scotch, looking in the mirror behind the bar she saw herself crying; she was too traumatized to know even she was crying. She downed her drink and poured another as she walked to their Jacuzzi adorned bathroom.

She stepped over to her IPod and pushed play, starting the Jacuzzi she poured the bottle of scotch and honey bubble bath cleanser into her water. The World's an Addiction by Nas and Anthony Hamilton finally came through the speakers, as she lowered herself into the hot alcohol infested bubble bath. In her mind the Scotch will cleanse her; it will renew her from that night. Only her mind, could not stop haunting her, visions of her parents and her friends' parents doing unthinkable things to her, made her scrub her body violently with the combination of Scotch and honey.

She dunked her head under the water, and a million thoughts were rapidly entering her cleansing process.

What type of shit was going on in their high-class society, was this the price her parents had to pay to be wealthy, a Japanese immigrant and a Black woman fitting into White society where you sacrifice your child to sexually sadistic acts. Who idea was it her step-father's or mother's, had to be her stepfather because they were introduced into that community by him.

Did he have his biological daughter sacrificed? Had to, because once she was 18 she fled to college and never came back. She never understood as to why her stepfather made sure her bank account was full if she disowned him. She never heard her discuss her except when he found out she was killed in a drive-by while she was in college. After the funeral, she remembers all her step-sister's things were boxed up in their living room.

Tara found a note from her step-sister addressed to her, she guesses she never got the chance to mail it. All she could read before her step-father pulled it out of her hand was "Watch the in-house devils around you masked with rich and smiling faces. Watch what you eat and drink."

If hindsight were 20/20, she would have deciphered what she wrote and heeded her warning. But to her thirteen-year-old mind, she was thinking it was some Religious and diet tips she was trying to give her.

Coming up for air, eyes burning from the Scotch and her state of mind lost in a fog of revenge. Tara ended her cleansing with Eminem and Lil Wayne's' No Love, and that is just what was entering her mind. She had no love for her dead parents; she had no love for

166

her friends' parents or her teachers. Any and everyone who was in that room or associated with it must perish. In her head, that was the only way she will be truly clean is with their blood.

Ghost

"Noooooooo, she screamed out of her sleep. Breaking out in a cold sweat, she hurriedly surveyed her surroundings. Her pale skin was paler than usual; her bright blue eyes were now dull and red. The same dream haunted her, or should she say memory.

The memory of getting beaten and then forced at gunpoint to smoke crack by someone she loved, chained by someone she damn near worshiped, and made into a slave. His slave, it was not enough for him to have her as his girlfriend, it was not sufficient for him to have her heart, it wasn't enough for him to have her mind, he had to conquer and destroy her soul also.

He had to control her and what better way to do it then with a controlled substance. Crack!!!!!

Desperately running towards the bathroom to cleanse her of the nightmare she once lived. Scolding hot water cascaded over her skin, as she used the cloth to scrub soap into her skin. Think of something good, she willed herself. Think of someone who wants to see you survive. Think of Miss Emma, she conjured up her smiling brown face and a sense of peace came over her.

In the distance, she heard her cell ring, the sound of the ringtone she rushed out of the tub to answer it, "Hello!"

"Why are you so out of breath?" the caller laughed.

"I almost busted my ass running to the phone." Ghost smiled.

"What ass?" the female replied.

"Tis white girl got dunky bootie," Ghost told her in a fake Jamaican accent while she starts clapping her ass and twerking in her mirror.

"Your ass is twerking, aren't you?" She laughed. She knew her friend all too well.

"And you know thisssssssss mannnn!" Ghost laughed into the phone.

"Good, so you will not mind going where I need you to go." No laughter was in her voice now. It was all business as she continued, "The Underground Playgrounds is where you need to be. MG will direct you to where you need to audition. When you meet, Bone and Vega tell them who sent you. Understand?"

"All good."

"Thank you, once again.Ghost. "

"No, thank you. We are killing two birds with one stone."

"Enough said. I'm done" she said

"Two fingers," Ghost replied and hit the end button.

Her phone rung was indicating that she had a text. It read, "Stop twerking, no ass and change your look up. Lol"

Ghost smiled and continued to twerk her ass in the mirror, "Shit, P tripping, my ass is gone with the wind fabulous." She laughed as she twirled around like Kenya Moore.

Hours later

Ghost looked at herself in the mirror as she put her green contacts in her eyes. She had transformed herself into someone she didn't even recognize, but she looked damn good. Her once bleached blond hair was now a golden blond, her skin was tanned to a natural looking pigment, and her green eyes sat her new look off. Her mind wandered to the timid blue eyed white girl she used to be before she became the only white girl in a predominately black neighborhood.

The kick in the door came abruptly; she flew under the bed as her mother directed her too. Gunshots rang throughout their mobile home; screams were echoing off the walls, frightening a young Ghost to tears. Covering her mouth so her screams will not alert the intruders, her whole body shook out of fear. She heard bullets fly into the room she was hiding in breaking lamps, piercing the walls above her head, bullets flying through the door of her room. The ten-year-old went into the fetal position, still in fear, still shaking and still covering her mouth full of screams.

Where once chaos stood, quietness took over; the aftermath of a bloody peaceful mess was left. The bullets ceased, and the voices of the intruders took over. Sensing their distraction, she crept to the bullet holes in the door to look out. Two white men had her father on his knees with a gun in his mouth, pulling his head back by his long ponytail towering over him as if they were more powerful, mightier, more deserving than him. Ghost studied their faces; it was etched, damned near fused in her mind.

Her eyes scanned the room looking for her mother; she was sprawled out on the kitchen floor lifeless. She almost let out a whimper, a mere sound that could have ended her life.

They did not spare her father's life as she had hoped; she looked on as one man let her dad's hair loose, only for the second man to put a hole in his head. Satisfied that they had accomplished what they had come for, they exited the shattered home.

Noises outside of the home made her run back under the bed. Hammering was being done outside of her home; she peeked out from under the bed only to watch one of the killers board up her window. This act was done to every window from the outside until the house was airtight, she and the decaying bodies of her parents were preserved in the big rectangle box on six acres of farmland.

Ghost was imprisoned for days with her parents, the smell, oh my God; the smell in that house was unbearable. The turning of the knob was her life saver; there stood Miss Emma, speechless and waiting for her with open arms.

She had no clue how Miss Emma knew to come, but she was thankful. Therefore, she did not utter not one question to the sweet lady who sometimes came to visit mommy and daddy. She flew into her arms and never looked back.

That was until she met Miss Emma's son, eight years her senior. Miss Emma's son was doing a little time for selling drugs when Miss Emma rescued her from that bloody box of death. She should have heeded Miss Emma's warnings and pleads that was against the feelings her son had for Ghost.

He was damn near a grown ass man taking a liking to a child. He never touched her at first just showered her with everything as if she was his, not his sister, not his play sister and not even his woman but HIS.

Ghost thought she would have problems being the only white girl in the hood, especially when she developed a natural swag from the hood and she had no idea where she got this curvaceous body from, but she was happy her ass could compete with the other girls. She did not encounter any problems because of the family she was living with, that shit went over her head for a long time. But, soon she found out a lot more than she wanted to about the sweet lady that came to visit her parent's every week.

Her sixteenth birthday was the night that twenty-four-year-old Jerome took her virginity. It was her sixteenth birthday when Jerome took over her life. She was nineteen when he put the gun to her head and made her smoke a crack pipe.

The Crack Pipe night

Ghost had been hearing about Jerome's extreme love for women, high priced strippers, call girls and sack chasers. Jerome enjoyed paying for a bitch because he felt he was always in control if he paid the cost to be the boss. Jerome money was starting to accumulate because of Ghost; she gave him the idea of catering to everyone's addiction. Instead of dealing just crack, he dabbled in everything from prescription drugs to heroin.

Even though he cheated on her daily, he loved her, he was obsessed with Ghost, her haunting blues eyes, white-blond hair, pouty lips and her innocence bewildered him into feelings he never had for anyone.

175

He molded her into what he wanted in a woman, obedient, non-nagging, naïve, quick to please him and gave him anything he desired. She took a blind eye to any nigga looking her way, even when she was in school with boys her age. Jerome had kept close tabs on her; she always knew who owned her and that was the way he liked it.

"So, fucking what!" Jerome said as he popped whatever pill it was, that he washed down with a bottle of Vodka. Ghost watched him in awe as he walked around her tied up body. Some of his friends were around the table playing cards, drunk or high, or both laughing at Jerome's belittlement of Ghost. She had left him for a couple of days after she found him getting his dick sucked by some random chick on the side of their house. He hunted her down and dragged her back home, tied her to a chair and was now voicing that he did not give a fuck that she was at his mom's house.

She had been tied up to the chair since last night, fear of last night haunting her as she gazed off into its memory.

Jerome pointed the gun at her head, "Suck it. Suck it. Suck it like your life depends on it." He yanked her by her hair, "And believes me it does." He added

He took his hand and wiped a tear from her face, "Oh don't cry, baby. You did not think about crying when you stayed away from home for two days. Now, since you feel the need to be disobedient. I feel the need to make you want to be obedient. I feel the need for you to suck your way back into obedience." He cocked the gun and with a sinister growl he ordered, now suck it!"

Tears slid down her face as she saw the evilness in his eyes. She flicked the Bic lighter under the glass dick, and she sucked on it because her life did depend on it. He made her do that all night; it alternated between sucking his cock and sucking the glass dick all night. Her mouth was sore.

She jumped out of her memory back into more misery.

"You want to jump ship, cause a nigga needed his dick sucked. What was I supposed to wait for your white ass to get home from school? You want to see how a nigga really gets down! I pay for bitches to do what I tell them with no back talk. "He told her as he motioned for his boys to let the hos in the living room.

He usually waited for this part of the activities, until Ghost were upstairs asleep. He would forbid her to come downstairs while his partners were there. But, now he wanted to show her he could do what the fuck he wanted to do and dare her to say something.

He might not be paying Ghost directly for sex, but he was taking care of her that was cause enough for her to shut the fuck up and take whatever shit he slung her way. Tied up in the middle of the floor to a chair Ghost was stripped naked by paid hookers in front of an audience of men and the man whom she thought loved her.

Jerome untied Ghost's legs; he instructed the hookers to get naked, "You, he pointed to the cute yellow girl with the big titties, straddle her." She strutted over towards Ghost still wearing her black heels and straddled her, making sure she rubbed her pussy up against Ghost. Ghost felt betrayed by the sensation that caused between her legs.

"Yeah, just like that! Now, make her suck your titties. Don't worry she has no choice but to play along or she knows what she will get or won't get. "He laughed. The room was clueless, but Ghost knew all too well what he was referring to. Ghost pulled the girl's nipple in her mouth and sucked on them like her life depended on it.

"Yes, swallow those titties, Jerome encouraged as he massaged his dick through his pants. Jerome loved what he was seeing, made him wish he would have done it sooner. It was something about making a bitch do something she would never do otherwise, that made his dick harder than it has ever been. Jerome untied Ghost's hands, whispering in her ear, "Behave now or pay for it later." He told her.

Ghost knew he was going to make her suck his dick and the glass dick all night if she did not engage in his sick twisted fantasy of his. She was fucked into lesbianism; no man was allowed to touch her they were just there to watch. Secretly, Jerome was taping her, just for extra insurance to ensure her obedience. That night she knew she had to escape or stay his smoked out sex slave for as long as he wanted. But, hell came before she was able too.

On one of the nights of his little lesbian shows, one of his friends slide his dick into her, while one of Jerome's nasty ass whores was grinding on top of her. Despite Jerome's protest, the man wouldn't stop ramming into Ghost. Ghost could not get up she had the weight of two bodies on top of her. Without another warning, Jerome took his gun and shot the man in his head. His fun was over but her night had just begun.

He chained her to a stripper pole by her legs, in the basement for days after the incident. Apparently, Jerome felt it was her fault he had to kill his friend. Luckily for her Miss Emma became concerned when she kept asking her son where Ghost was, and he kept giving her different excuses.

Miss Emma took it upon herself to investigate; she used her spare key to go in her son's house. When she reached the basement she was in shock to see her adopted daughter chained to a pole, looking like hell, she was skinny, and her once beautiful blue eyes were sunken in and her skin ashy. Miss Emma dropped to her knees in front of Ghost with tears of shame in her eyes.

Miss Emma rose up and pulled out her .360 and shot the chain off of her. She hated what her son did to her; she tried to stop it from happening, but Ghost was too hard headed to listen to her. She had raised this little girl for damn near ten years and under her care, this is what happened to her.

This is what she exposed her to, Miss Emma ran through the house like a mad woman, getting things together for Ghost. She dressed her, sat her in the car. Then Miss Emma went back in and threw gasoline everywhere and lit that motherfucker up with her Virginia Slim.

In the car, Miss Emma confessed to making the call to have her parents killed, yes she could have saved them from Jerome, but she had wanted Ghost all to herself. She loved the little girl, and she thought she deserved better than two crackheads as parents. Ghost's parents sold crack to the whites in their part of town. Money kept being off and Jerome wanted them dead.

Miss Emma told him she did not care do what he had to do, but leave the little girl alone and alive. The two goons he sent there that night did not see Ghost, so they followed through with Jerome's plans. Her young son was running things in their small town, thanks to Miss Emma's brother. Miss Emma had to check for herself, so she went to the house, and there she found a horrified, lonely and starved little girl.

She drove Ghost where she could get a car and gave her money for gas, and told her to get as far away from the state of Michigan as quick as she can. She then she broke ties with Miss Emma and went away to join Atterbury Job Corps. But she would never forget, what she told her in the car. Ghost might have been out of it, but she was coherent enough to

182

understand that from the beginning Jerome was the Devil, who started her hell.

To Jerome's knowledge Ghost died in that fire. He felt guilty, but not guilty enough to stop doing what the fuck he wanted to do to women.

Now, she was twenty-five, the nightmare of her parents being killed in front of her was still fresh in her mind and so was the hell Jerome took her through. Her hell and her nightmare were connected, it was all associated, and she would seek her bittersweet revenge. The one thing she knew would probably never change about him is he loved paying for sex, she had her own plan. And who better to help her orchestrate her plans than Black Panther, herself.

She was staying at a hotel in Indianapolis, where she was contacted to because evidently this Bone nigga (Pantha told her about) had beef with Jerome also and he knew how to get to him.

Spanish fly

"Dimly lit, less than up to par motel room.
Grotesque ROOM!" She yelled in her thick Spanish
accent at the four walls, as she raised her gin bottle
up to the ceiling of a dimly lit, less than up to par
motel room.

"¿Cómo pueden ir Contra familia. Mi Familia, mi
culo. She spoke into her bottle of gin, MS 13 was
tattooed on the inner part of her wrist it was a fatal
signature inked into her skin, and this is the tattoo
of the Mara Salvatrucha, one of Latin America's
largest street gangs. Death, blood, and Nihilist
rebellion are their territory in her home of El
Salvador.

A decision that was made for her, a life she did
not choose to live. A night of holy terror, she was
unwillingly penetrated and branded at the same time.
In result of this night, three things stayed with her,
the memory, the tattoo, and her 3-month-old son.
Except for her son, because, "Los pendejos de mierda

dejan ese fucker tomar mi bebé." She muttered as she staggered to the little kitchen in the motel room, she lit her cigar and with a non-sober sway she caught a glimpse of herself in the mirror attached to the back of the bathroom door.

She stared at her reflection; she pulled on the cigar to watch the exhaling of the smoke come from her nostrils. She saw the devil in herself, adorned in all red, her lips red; her bra and panty set red, her heels red and her eyes were even bloodshot red. Swaying from side to side she felt her milk come down like her son was crying for her. Crying for her to feed him as he always did. As the milk soaked her bra and dropped from her bosom, tears drowned her eyes in its wetness. The milk would not stop coming down; it was days of build up from not being able to feed her son. "Mi niño Lo siento. Siento. Siento. "She cried.

After being held down and raped, her family talked her into not going to the police. But on top of that, on top of that degrading act, her family let the man who raped her come and snatch her son away from her. All so they can get the funds to go to America.

It was not enough for her to be brutally raped, they destroyed the only thing that made her cope with her rape, they only good that came out of it, was her beloved son.

She remembers dropping to her knees, so she dropped while still holding on to the gin bottle, she remembered begging, screaming, crying for someone in her family to not let that Diablo take her child. She held onto Diablo's leg, even though with each kick she became bloodier, with each stomp she became bruised she still did not dare let go of him. She let him drag her across rocks and broken glass, hoping that this would show him the depths of which she would go through to keep her son. If God's acts didn't mean shit to the devil, what made her think her actions meant shit to him.

Neighbors holding their hearts, the tears of the neighboring mothers sympathized with her as they prayed and did the cross sign while holding their Rosaries. You had people to look on in fear and disgust, cursing Diablo out under their breath; some not even brave enough to do that because the devil hears all. However, no one came to her and her son's aide. No one intervened, not even the police officer's that threw her into the back of a truck.

She rode away watching the tears of her family; they did not mean shit to her. She threw up her middle finger at them, at everyone she passed that was gawking and looking and not helping, all because the man who was doing this to her was the Diablo the head of Mara Salvatrucha. Diablo will not be seeing the last of her.

Her family did not see the last of her either; that was why she was drowning herself in gin, hoping the effects of it will numb her completely, erase her memories of why her bloody outfit was soaking in a tub full of bleach in an American city called Indianapolis.

ROC VEGA

"Check these bitches' houses and cars. If that shit is trifling, then their snatches are trifling. I'm not power washing none of these hoes' snatches with disinfectant and I'm not in the business of selling dirty cunts." Roc Vega disconnects his call, and glares at the group of naked women spread eagle before him and his men.

Walking strategically down the line, he inhales his Kush smoke while observing each female with gloves on. He examines them like he was their Gynecologist. He stops in his tracks as a smell overpowers the aroma of his Kush.

"Oh hell naw! Get this dirty pussy broad out of my presence. Smelling like Hoarders need be knocking on her fucking pussy lips." He hollered out in disgust. The men yanked the female in question up by her weave and escorted her out.

Roc Vega turns to Bone, "My Nig, you need to get some snatch sniffing dogs so we can smell these hoes before they even set foot in the building."

Bone couldn't do shit but laugh at his ass. He knew it was the right choice to bring him into the Underground Playground nobody knew pussy and Kush like Vega and with La La, who made pole dancing an art form, this was looking like a profitable revenge plot.

Outside, the undesired chick threw herself to her knees, forcefully and quickly undid the pants of the man who was escorting her out, pulling out his manhood, she had to get in on this and if she had to suck this wildebeest brains through his fucking dickhole, so be it.

Vonda pulled her hair to the side and inch by inch; she inhaled this nigga's sweaty putrid penis, now isn't this about a bitch. She proceeded, back in the building as she thought her interactions were being recorded and watched. Vega watched in amusement, as he watched his boy's reactions to her fellatio skills.

Roc Vega laughed, watching the screen with Jah, "She swallowed the whole package, no chestnuts or chin nuts." Jah smirked at Vega to see what he was going to do.

"With skills like that, guess a nigga will have to do some power washing today." Vega chuckled as he blew smoke from his mouth.

"Nigga, don't act like your ass hasn't run into some bad pussy. Matter fact, nigga that one bitch from back in the day that lived in those apartments on 5th Ave." Jah said trying to jog Vega's memory.

"Bone, you got the wrong motherfucker. I don't fuck with unexceptional hoes. Now, let's get back to business." Vega said trying to change the subject.

"Hell No, nigga did you just attempt to change the subject?" Jah followed Vega out of the surveillance room.

Vega was going to run Bone's pussy resume to him except La La interrupted, "I need to talk to you, she said talking to Jah and she walked into his office.

"Damn, what you do to La? She about to whoop your ass like she used to when we were younger." Vega laughed

"Shut up, with your brown ass," Jah said walking back towards his office.

La La didn't waste any time as soon as she heard the door open she had her hands on her thick hips, "What's up, with finding out what happened to Que?"

Jah had a bad feeling that his little sister was about to find out some shit she wasn't ready to handle. That was why he was trying to keep her occupied with running the pole dance classes, the exercise classes, and the dance classes. She was like the Den mother at a sorority house.

Jah took a minute to assess carefully what to do first. Some of those men who was at the house looked like professionals, but he could be wrong. The best way to find out about a nigga is to go to his hometown and find out what he did in his past that he doesn't want his future to know. "We will head to Gary before the Grand revised opening."

"You already know who to question, don't you?" La La accused him with an attitude.

"Lose the attitude, Lalita. He told her as he walked past her to sit at his desk. He opened up a drawer pulled out a cigar and lit it, dressed in a charcoal gray Kenzo T-shirt, charcoal gray Timbs, and True Religion gray tinted blue jeans.

"As far as I'm concern that nigga can stay right where he is, stinking or hiding. With that said you need to prepare yourself for the worst, and you need to go back to your house, so you can walk me through what happened that day." He pointed to the door as if he was dismissing her; La La stuck up her middle finger at Jah. Jah laughed at his sister because he used to do that when they were younger to let her know she needed to leave. She hated it then being five years younger than him, and she despised it now.

La La kept her mouth shut Gary was a long ride to start an argument with a man who can hold a grudge for years. She went back to the living quarters of the house to pack her belongings. Ghost knocked on the door to the La La's room from the adjoining bathroom they shared.

"Karen," La answered the knock by calling Ghost by her government name.

"Lalita, Ghost sarcastically replied back stepping into her room.

Ghost sat on La's Chaise Lounge sitting at the end of her marble four posted canopy bed. When La looked up, Ghost was dressed in a Vintage sheer champagne-colored 1920's dress, finger waves with headband and feather. "Damn, girl! You sure you are not mixed with African American." La always commented on that Ghost looked mulatto and not fully white.

"All my life I had two white parents." Ghost replied like always. She watched La La pack her bags and not once did she ask her anything.

"So, are you going to ask me?"

196

"Nope, I figured if you wanted me to know you would tell me." Ghost told her crossing her legs.

La gave a smirk and nodded her head, like she agreed with Ghost's logic. "So, when I get back I need you to take a ride with me."

"Cool, let me go. I have a request to dance, and this is the costume they desire", she said posing. "5,000 to fan dance for some old ass white men. Oh, yo girl is about to get her Josephine Baker on." She said jingling her pale slightly voluptuous ass. That girl could put a smile on anyone's face; La La thought to herself.

Gangsta Island

"You shouldn't have married that fucking riff raff, in the first place," Jah told La La as they just finished putting two in one of Que's enemies he had accumulated before he met La La. Que had a price on his head in his hometown of Gary, Indiana. She knew that but not for the reasons his ass made it be.

The true Que felt as if the world owed his ass something for spending 11 years in jail. This nigga thought he was a revolutionary, a black rebel, who somehow was a fucking political prisoner wrapped up in a damn gangster rapper all in his own head. In actuality, this nigga was just a fucked up individual.

He wanted a pat on the back, a car, house, the red carpet, rap contract, clothes, etc. Just because he did something in the life, he was trying to live; that was part of the code. The street code. No snitching. Usually, when an organization picks someone to take the fall, that person is usually the less valuable within its organization. Que felt like he was the realest brother in the world.

"I'm just not the only motherfucker in the G that wants that nigga gone. If I find that nigga, believe me, I'm killing his ass and hosting a parade with his body on the float. Que is a grimy ass fuck boy. That nigga whole claim to street fame is larceny, shit he used to steal from our mother and her many boyfriends. You guys might want to vouch for a different motherfucker, and you might want to get your ass out of the G speaking that nigga's name. I'm his brother, and I don't even fuck with him." Even with two masked gunmen with their guns to his head did not stop him from telling the truth about his brother. La La gave David her number before they exited his car.

Jah did not give a fuck about Que; he was doing this shit for his sister. As they got, Que's brother added, "By the way, that nigga not dead or kidnapped. I would have heard about it by now. I don't mean to be harsh, but you are going to end up killing that nigga when you find him, or you are not going to find him. Rest assured his grimy ass did some shit to you, you just haven't found out what it is yet." He laughed as he went on his way.

Just before they hit the highway to go to Chicago Midway Airport, La La phone vibrated with a text, Check social networks and anything dealing with his computer. He never deletes his history. La La assumed that was Que's brother. She forgot about everything at home. She needed to go back like Jah said.

The underground

playgrounds

The expensive motorcycles were placed
strategically throughout the warehouse with each girl
dressed in crotchless sexy motorcycle outfits. The
girls submitted their bodies to The Weeknd's Wicked
Games; each girl was in sync with the other,
committing each muscle to the erogenous sound of the

voice satiating the air with words that every man in that warehouse wanted to say.

The motorcycles had strap-on placed upward on the seats, stripper poles were placed securely by the bikes. These were Clientele that loved to ride expensive bikes, loved to fuck expensive bitches and loved the expensive feel of just one clicking without the pain of having to worry about how much they had.

Collectively each girl positioned themselves above the seat of the bike; the crowd came closer and closer, enthralled with the thought of these women fucking the motorcycles. Images of these exotic looking women dancing on their Johnsons flashed through their minds.

Each girl did as they rehearsed a thousand times, enticing them with the arch of their backs, mouths, yearning for their wetness dripping down the shaft of the strap-on onto the seats. It was a combination of stripping, professional dance and porn.

La La covered in all tailored black suit created to fit the curves of her body; it was a sexy outfit but all business. She watched on as a proud mother watching how the ladies were in sync with each other, steady enticing each male to go deeper into his pockets. Shit, this was worth every penny, watching a sexy bitch fuck a sexy bike was worth more than a penny and La could not wait to get her cut.

As La watched on she spotted a familiar face, what seemed to be familiar to her, but he had dreads and a different nose. She was trying to get closer without being obvious, but someone nigga stepped in her way.

Jah already made sure all men knew the price range of each show this one, in particular, was 20 bills and up. He didn't want to see two $10 or four $5; it had to be 20 dollar bills and up.

He was working on getting the girls phones that charged credit cards; their percentage would go into one account, and his cut went to his account. Their credit card bill would say UPS as in Underground Playgrounds.

Jah and Vega were admiring La La's handy work, Envy had the idea but Jah had the vision, and his sister and Vega were helping him put it into fruition. He caught a glimpse of his sister and followed her eyes' to some dude in dreads. Just like La, to him, he looked familiar. Jah starts walking towards him, but when dread head saw La coming towards him, he tried to dart out of there.

Speaking into his headpiece, Jah whispered some orders. The man on the other end started the car up as he saw Dread head hightail it to his vehicle. He followed him to the gas station; Gab filled up as the man filled up. Gab also grabbed some snacks because the man grabbed some snacks. To him this indicated that this ride was going to be long, he needed to be prepared.

Dread head and Gab both filled up next to each other; Gab ear hustled as the scared as fuck boy screamed into the phone, "Y'all motherfuckers are trying to get me killed. You said you killed her."

"What the fuck ya mean, who is this?" Dread head snapped into the phone. He finished pumping his gas, opened up his passenger door and got in the car.   Gab could see that Dread's were still fussing at whoever. He was trying to see who was driving, shit she looked good as hell. He saw Dread hang the phone and grab the chick by the hair for a deep kiss.

Gab hung his nozzle up, put his cap back on and got into his car and pulled off. He hid his vehicle on the side where a little dirt road was, as soon as Dread's passed him, he pulled off behind him. He watched as the girl went down on Dreads while he steered the car. Gab shook his head and grabbed his gun. His cell started ringing; he viewed the caller's information, "Answer, he commanded.

"Where?" Jah asked

"Bone, you got a nigga taking a damn road trip," Gab said!

"I got you, my nigga. About where?" Jah reassured him.

"We headed up north, but we are in the boondocks, where niggas probably are hanging from trees," Gab told him.

Hours later they arrived in Michigan, in some small city on the border of Indiana and Michigan.

As the couple walked into the house to retire, Gab eased his way onto and into their vehicle to set up bugging devices and camera under the driver seat so he could see between that beautiful ass bitch's legs.

Gab noticed that no one stopped to turn off an alarm, matter of fact he didn't even think he saw them unlock the door with a key. Must be nice to live where you do not have to lock your door, and then again he probably thought his home was above being touched. Gab thoughts would be right Dreads thought his home was above being touched.

The next morning Gab watched as both Dreads and his woman got in the car. He watched the dirt road; it was only three houses on that street, and they were all spread apart. So, just walking up to the house and getting in should be a cinch.

Gab searched throughout the house and placed bugs in the places where people have the most conversations at, the kitchen, living room, bedroom, and bathroom. He continued to search the house; he came to the basement door it was locked.

"What the hell?" Gab said to himself. He couldn't believe this simple motherfucker, you keep your front door unlocked but lock your basement door. Automatically, a person knew that the basement had some shit in it, shit that needed to be protected.

Gab paused, instead of picking the lock on the steel door, he placed a small camera above the door and facing the door. He needed to know, how far this nigga would go to protect what was behind that steel door. He could be walking his ass right into a trap. He would have to hold off until he knew more about this motherfucker here.

Gab headed his ass back to Indiana, keeping track of what was going on through his state of the art Tablet. It was about midnight when he saw, who he now knew as Naomi, get undressed with her back to the camera. Gab was happy he was back in the comfort of his own apartment. He pulled his dick out as he saw Naomi's voluptuous yellow ass sitting nice and high.

The bathroom became steamy from the hot water, but Naomi was still visible. He watched as she lathered up her sponge, caressing the sponge over her breast, then her arms, just as she bent over, Dreads came in butt naked behind her and kept her bent over as he drilled her ass, Gab moved the camera to get a close-up on Naomi's face. He wanted to jack off to her beautiful ass not a nigga fucking her.

Dreads washed his dick off and left Naomi to finish with her cleaning, Gab was just about to nut when the door being opened eliminated some of the steam. Gab's hand flew to his mouth as he threw up chunks when he saw the girl of his dreams washing her dick.

Meanwhile,

La La flew back home undetected with Ghost; She knew Jah's mind was occupied with something, and she took advantage of that. Her brother couldn't lie to her; she could tell him, and Gab had something going on and he had something to do with the look alike that popped up and the UPS.

La La house was sitting on land, property that she owned right out, and she paid cash. She did not have neighbors for at least a mile or two. She loved her secluded area. She entered her home, taking notice of the replaced windows and flooring. She walked to the house where she knew bullet holes should have been; there was not any.

One thing she did notice was that everything else was untouched, the way she left her bedroom and her kitchen was the same. Everything was the same; there was not any sign of a struggle except for the altercation she had in the bedroom. La La knew Jah must have done that on purpose, so she could recall everything that happened that night.

So, why wasn't there any sign of a struggle in any other part of the house? There was no way that Que could have been taken from the bedroom, without her being awoken. Come to think of it, with all of the guns she strategically had hidden around the house. There should have been a struggle some fucking where other than that bedroom.

La La grabbed Ghost, "Follow me! As Ghost followed La La, she poured her soul out about what happened and what was going on. "I don't want to tell my brother, but I don't think that bastard was kidnapped. I think this was a tactic just to get out of our marriage. But the thing I can't figure is, why do it this way?"

"Yeah, Ghost chimed in, why not just tell a bitch it's not working out?"

"Shit, because that's too much like right." La La laughed. They made their way to the office, "Okay, I'll check the laptop, and you check the computer on the desk." She pointed.

"I do not know what your husband did but, he had taste." Ghost told her as she sat behind the cherry wood Del Mar U-Shape Executive Desk with Hutch.

"I had all this before he came into the picture!" La La confessed. Opening up his laptop, his screen saver was their wedding picture. She quickly typed in the password, went straight to the files. Nothing was in the archives but as soon as she went to the internet and to the history. You can tell no one has tampered with the laptop; the last history was the same day everything happened.

They say one's history is important, this shit shifted everything the other way. This shit right here was about to get a motherfucker killed. "In the top drawer is a cigar box full of weed. Do you know how to roll?" La La got her answer when Ghost started rolling up. She set the laptop down, went to another side of the room, pushed a button and a door slide open to reveal a bar. She fixed her a double shot of Diva Vodka with a cap full of papaya juice. She held up the bottle to Ghost, she shook her head no and pointed to the Bollinger Champagne. La La grabbed a bottle and gave it to her.

Ghost gave her the blunt and La lit it, grabbing his laptop she motioned for Ghost to follow her down some hidden stairs behind a curtain in the office. Waving her hand over this silver thing another door slide open, they walked downstairs to a plush all black apartment.

La La set the laptop down and continued to walk up some stairs where light cascade all around an all-black bedroom suite that filled the whole layout of the top floor with all black marble bathroom.

Ghost was not going to show it, but she was impressed. She had to give La La her boss fedora; no one else had one except for P. That was a salute she gave women who made it on their own without a nigga. This gave her the confidence that she could have everything she wanted and get it on her own, without a man given it to her.

La La turned on Freedom from the Django soundtrack as she lit the blunt and took a sip of her drink. The coldness and sweetness of the drink ran down her unquenched throat, a throat that was holding a scream that was looking for freedom.

Her mind relaxed, the alcohol and cannabis helped her conjure up an incident that happened before she met her husband. What made her vulnerable to this type of nigga? It wasn't shit particular about Que? He seemed verbal, not intelligent. What happened to make her slip up enough to let this type of nigga even around her?

La La set straight up in bed and passed Ghost the blunt. She gulped down her drink and unsuppressed the memory she had been burying for years.

Suppressed memory

La was closing up one of Jah's establishments in ATL, while he dealt with the death of Jazzy. She was closing up all of the offices because it was about to be the weekend. She had a steel briefcase full of this week's benefits, as she did for the last month.

La phone rung, "Yes! I know you are down the block hit the elevator." Just as she hung up a sound startled her and made her look behind her; she was eye to eye with some suicidal masked man. Quickly, La La realized she was too close to him to pull her gun. She hurriedly swung the briefcase connecting with her assailant's nose.

La La made the biggest of mistake of her life, she didn't kill him like she was supposed to, still lying on the floor the masked man grabbed La by her feet, lunging her body onto the floor. She flipped her body over on her back and kicked him in the face as he pounced toward her, knocking him sideways. Taking advantage of him being dazed, she got up to run to the back stairs, only to be hit from behind. She passed out after several hits but she knew she heard more than one voice laughing at the nigga she put on the floor.

She awoke in the hospital unable to move without wincing. Gab and her brother were by her side, after she told him what she knew. Jah went to work trying to find out who did that to his sister. But all she could remember was the long dreads under that mask and those eyes. Two weeks later is when she met Que. He came in her room by accident looking for his friend. They struck up a conversation and he lead La La to believe that he used to be in the streets, but now he was in partner with a friend doing legal things.

She remembered now when she first met Que he had contacts in, claiming to have poor eyesight without them. High and tipsy she had an epiphany, she shot straight up off the bed. Ghost was telling her story, La heard her through her thoughts but did not respond yet. She could not, not with this newfound information.

La La walked back downstairs, this time, she did not care if Ghost followed or not. She was feeling some type of way, a way that if she came across Que right now, she would be too happy to chop his dick off, blend it in the blender and feed it to the fucking dogs at his crackhead ass mother's house.

Ghost followed her downstairs to finish what she started; she had printed out all of Lalita's bank information how one account with her husband's name on it had activity from Michigan, and it was damn near depleted. That account just happens to be the account she opened up, and the both of them had been putting money into it. Trust is a dangerous fucker when given to the wrong person.

Que had stolen his own child's money and so now she knew that motherfucker in the Underground was that nigga. La La went through all his accounts; he had been lying to females talking about how he had a concert in their hometown coming up soon. And what was more horrific is that some of those females had dicks and that fuck boy knew they had dicks. The things she had read about him and Naomi, their relationship was deeper than rest. That shit also made her feel some level of disgust. This nigga was running the same shit to me as he was doing to He/She. She also found out he lied and said that La La and their son had died in a house fire recently.

There was even a messages on FB between him and her and a lot of other females. He even joined unique sex groups for men who like trannies. She made her a fake Facebook page, and screen shot all of Que's dirt

216

that was during their relationship and sent it to her.

Some of it were as recent as this morning. Now, all

she needed to do was wait to see what Naomi would do.

Jah & La

What the hell is going on in this fucking world,
Jah thought as he read all the information La sent him
through email. What kind of men was the devil sending
to destroy his world? He knew it; he knew it, he
fucking knew that nigga Que was a bitch. This
coincides with Gabe's footage of the dread head dude.
La and Jah sat in his office going through all of
Que's emails, profiles to social and dating websites.

Going through his pictures she came upon his
pictures and looked as far back as two years, and
there it was, she clutched her hands together. An
image of Que in a mask with his dreads hanging out,
that was the nigga who had a part in robbing her. Her
eyes had tears, tears of anger not so much towards Que
but at herself.

Jah saw the angry tears, "La, I know you are not
crying over this bitch ass nigga's shenanigans?"

La looked at him through slits, "No, nigga, she said and just pointed to the screen. Before he could get over there, La pushed her chair back and walked to the bar. "Dread Head is about to be no more," She said as she poured herself and Jah a glass of spirits. He looked at the picture confused but took the glass from her and took a sip of the brown liquor.

"That's the motherfucker who robbed me!" La pointed to the picture of Que.

Jah started shaking his head and downed his drink. "Yeah! Yeah! That nigga has to die." He said as he walked over to his desk to his cell phone. La got a notification that she had an email from her fake account.

"No. Let me handle it and let me handle it my way. Book me a flight to Detroit, now." La said smiling as she read her Facebook inbox, she grabbed her keys and left.

La and Naomi

La met Naomi at the Jazz Café in Detroit,
Michigan. Naomi was taller than La and slimmer; you
could not tell she was a man. The scarf around her
neck made sure of that. La walked in with a curvaceous
sway, dominating the attention of everyone including
her potential enemy depending on how this meeting
went.

Naomi stood up unconsciously, shook La's hand and
sat after she sat. Well, damn even the confused
recognize I'm a fucking lady. Naomi did not have
anything against transgender per say, just this one.
Not because she had her faggot ass husband, it was
because this bitch probably was wearing her son's
money.

Pulling off her sunglasses La smiled, "Let's get down to the point. I don't give a fuck about that nigga. I climbed in bed with a nigga I shouldn't have, end of fucking story. But, what I do give a fuck about, what I would kill a nigga for is this little boy right here, she showed Naomi her screen saver of her son on her phone, she continued, "And anything and everything that belongs to him is included. Which leads me to why I contacted you, your boyfriend Que stole money from my son, and I want you to get it back for me." La told her as she summoned for the waiter.

Naomi thought in her head; this bitch is fierce, she had to smile to himself. Yeah, that nigga Que had to make sure he was a totally different man to be with this bitch. Not the want be fucking thug, won't be intelligent, I'm pro-black, but I hit women because I'm weak, trifling ass. Naomi thought all this to herself as she flung off her classes.

"Just as long as a bitch get paid, Sweetie, Hook or Crook I'm with you to get revenge on that motherfucker. You see this, Naomi said, pointing to the bruises on her face. "This is my money boo. I'm going, to be honest with you; I fuck with ballers that like their ass and dick served in a feminine package. I thought Que was, but that nigga came into my life under false fucking pretenses. Waving money but not spending shit, I was doing all the spending, like a dumb ho. I told myself I would never fall in love with a nigga who wasn't honest about his sex life." Naomi confessed

La La couldn't ridicule Naomi for that shit; after all, she married the bum ass nigga. She actually felt apologetic, as if she created Que and sent him for him/her. There was no way in hell Que would have put his hands on her and live to tell about it, so she was going to feed her more hate, to keep her loyalty until she was done with Que. She knew she was motivated by money, so she was going to present her with a healthy sum.

La was quiet, not showing her hand. "Well, let's get this nigga. Evidently you know the real Que, so I need to know how can you get me close to him?" La inquired.

"This nigga always wanted to have a threesome bringing in a woman, who would be down to fuck both of us. Are you going to pay somebody else to go in with me?" Naomi questioned.

"Hell no, I want to do this myself. " La La smiled deviously

"Well, you must have one hell of a disguise. Because that nigga has pictures of you plastered on the walls in the basement. That is why I look like this. Yeah, I went in the forbidden place. For the last year, I have never been allowed in that fucking basement. After you had sent me all that information, I had to get into that basement. I might have gotten

my ass beat for being in there, but you better believe
a bitch came out with something. " Naomi beamed as she
pulled out information on an account that Que had over
75 g's stashed.

La looked over the information and found her name
on the account also; this must have been one of the
papers he had her sign that day when she thought she
was signing for the account for her son. This nigga
had to open an account with her name his bad credit
having ass. So that means she can just waltz her love

If this bitch thinks I'm not about to get revenge
on this nigga she silly as hell, La La thought. She
waited to see what she was about to say before; she
voiced what she was thinking.

Naomi ordered another drink to calm her nerves.
Que was certifiable nut job; she read his prison
psychology report. If she would have gotten a hold to

those documents before she would have been gone. If this did not go right, she knew he would be after her.

"So, when do you want me to set it up? At least, give me a week to get back into his good graces, get everything back to normal. You can trust me; money always is the motivation." Naomi reassured her.

"Keep me posted. But the sooner, the better, that way you can spend your money and live a happy, comfortable life. And my soul will be at peace knowing I did not let that nigga fuck over my son." La La said as she paid the bill. She discreetly reached into her purse and pulled out an envelope with 10 g's in it and slides it on the table towards Naomi. Naomi beamed; La La knew that sealed Que's fate. That nigga Que was as good as gone.

La la

As her son lay peacefully in his crib, La La sat on the bed with tears of hate in her eyes, tears that could easily affect you like a snake's venom. She loaded her gun with the platinum and diamond bullets that were made from the melted down jewelry her so called husband had given her over the years.

Now that she knew the truth, the love that she once had for her husband was replaced by a deep dark hatred. She reflected back to her actions over the past year in the Underground Playground trying to find out who kidnapped him or possibly who killed him, the blood that was on her hands all in the name of "Que"!

How quickly a lying, deceitful, selfish motherfucker can make a thin line between love and hate completely disappears, as if love was never there.

After her task was complete, La La walked across the darkly lit room and kissed her son on the forehead. She admired how much he looked like Que, stroking the curls upon his little head, she whispers, "Sorry, Baby Boy your daddy must have forgotten, I'm not the type of woman you fuck over!" La La grabs her hoody, places the guns in the small of her back and walks out into the foyer where everyone is standing.

Jah walked up to her, "You sure you want to give that nicca his jewelry back?"

"Every last piece!" she commented

He nodded, understanding where she was coming from, "Alright, you know I'm with you!" La La, Jah, and Vega walked out the house and got into the truck to drive her to her destination. This was a mission La La wanted to do on her own; this was personal. Her heart was fucked up, and she didn't like that feeling.

"All, I have to say is fucking with your ass La, a bitch would never get a piece of jewelry from me!" Vega admitted. The three of them laughed at his comment, "I'm just saying, Ma, you cold for this one. I'm impressed." he continued as they were reaching the rental car.

"A good girl can turn into a bad girl! A bad girl can turn into a cold-hearted bitch!" She told them as she put her leather gloves on. She left them with that as she made her way to her rental. She plugged her IPod into the radio; "Hard to Breathe by Violetz Are Blue" filled the speakers! That is exactly what La La was going to do, make it hard for that nicca to breathe!

Jah and Roc Vega watched as La La pulled off but revenge was driving that car, you could tell by the trail of dust she left in the air. "Damn Bone, this shit almost make me not want to treat these hos wrong," Vega said shaking his head almost believing himself.

"Yeah, right nicca! "Jah laughed, besides hos and bitches you're supposed to treat wrong. That's a real woman; they're not even in the same category! Shit, a motherfucker, gone learn today!" He pulled off in the opposite direction to handle his own business.

La la

La entered the room with Naomi right beside her; the darkness surrounded her, transforming her revenge into something so evil Lucifer himself, would have to fall to his knees and pray to God. Halloween, the night in which masks were welcoming and the sight of death dressed in thigh-high boots, fishnet stockings, with an unbelievable sensual sheer leotard all covered up in an onyx hooded mantle and adorned a scythe in her right gloved hand was customary.

Que watched in carnal astonishment, as he silently gave Naomi her props for picking this one out, she was the worst bitch he has seen thus far. She was thick in all the right places. He listened to the sound of her heels penetrating the marble floor; he watched as she swung her cloak open to expose the front of her body, the muscles in her thighs flexed with every step.

"Damn left his lips as he watched his masked Grim Reaper reach her destination of the iPod, the speakers bellowed an eerie, erotic beat with an, even more, sensual spine-chilling voice.

Naomi just stood there waiting to do her part; she watched as La went to each French door and opened them, leaving the onyx curtains to rage through the doors from the wind. The wind threatening to blow out the black candles that were lit around the room made for an enjoyable atmosphere, one might think romantic, one might believe that this woman went out of her way to create this for the man she loves. One might think the screams being covered up by the rain; wind and music are cries of passion. That one motherfucker was wrong as La tied Que ass upward on the bed.

She walked over to Naomi as she grabbed her mantle by the neck and threw it on the floor, Naomi handed her the specially made strapon, careful not to grab it by the shaft La put it on carefully. Que was anticipating what nasty shit Naomi and this sexy ass Grim Reaper had in store for him.

La grabbed the alcohol and the cocaine and poured it all over the shaft of the strap-on. Naomi set the bag down and walked over to La, Naomi put a condom on her penis before she entered Que, Que bucked at first, and he couldn't believe that Naomi violated his asshole. He had dealt with a lot of transsexuals, but he was the man, not the fucking woman so he did not and was not supposed to get fucked in the ass.

However after a while, Que was throwing his ass back at Naomi, wanting Naomi to go deeper. La shook her head, this faggot ass motherfucker. Her thoughts deepened her hate as Naomi increased her strokes in Que's ass. This nigga was probably sucking fucking dick and then coming home to her, kissing her all in the mouth and on her stomach while she was pregnant. This lying motherfucker was talking about he doesn't like anal sex and he getting fucked in the ass. Rage overtook her, whatever plan she had to prolong this shit, went out the window.

La yanked Naomi by the arm; Naomi looked confused. Nevertheless, Naomi removed her penis from Que and stepped back. La placed a blue scarf around his mouth; Que did not question it, and he has been gagged before. La made sure the ropes were tight; she placed her hand on the headboard, exposing the second half of his heart tattoo.

Que's eyes widened as he saw the tattoo, La watched his recognition, and she entered him without even touching her razor embellished simulated penis. She slowly went in and out as the razors searched for flesh to puncture. La looked at his head he was throwing it back, forward, and side to side, she reached for his dreads and pulled him backward so she could see his face. The absolute horror on his face put a smile on her face. She felt blood pour down her legs as she fucked him slowly. She would not dare fuck the shit out of him when it was clear she was trying to seduce his ass to death with each slice of the razor blade.

Visions of shit set off in La La's head, like bombs. Each stroke became harder and more powerful than the last; she reached in the back of her where the holsters were located. La La came forward with both guns aiming at the back of his head, without missing a stroke she gave her late husband every piece of jewelry he ever gave her. La felt his body grow rigid; she made a sound like she was nutting, pulled out and told Que's corpse, "I hope that was as good for you as it was for me." She laughed and smacked him on the ass.

Naomi could not even find the words to explain what she just witnessed, La La was humming as she undressed to take a shower and jump into her other outfit for tonight. When she got out Naomi was still standing in the same spot. La walked over to her and snapped her fingers; she saw the look in Naomi's eyes, those were eyes that couldn't handle what just took place, Naomi's eyes held the look of a potential snitch.

La walked to the bag and pulled out a pair of plastic black overalls, gloves and then she threw the same to Naomi. Naomi feared touching Que's dead body, but she was more terrified of La La. She continued to his body trying her damnedest not to touch any part of him while she was untying him.

Uncomplainingly, La waited for Naomi to finish her task, she walked over to Que's body ready to pick him up and carry him to the Jacuzzi tub big enough for six people. Quickly the girls took him to the bathroom and slung him into the tub; his body hit it with a thud. Naomi continued to stare at Que's body; she once loved this man whom he thought loved him as herself.

La observed Naomi as she walked up behind him/her, she swung the scythe down on Naomi's neck, her head rolled as blood squirted from her neck and her torso fell right on top of Que's. Naomi must have forgotten that she was still her enemy. Besides female or male Naomi was a weak bitch that would get her ass put under the jail.

La La changed the song on her Ipod and turned it up loudly Nas' voice echoed through the house as he rapped about needing only One Mic; she slashed down on Que's limbs taking pride in her butchering skills.

After three hours of One Mic on repeat, two bodies chopped up and incinerated. She opened all the windows and doors of the section of the house; she sprayed the bathroom with the cleaning solution that they clean crime scenes. She sprayed the bed down even though she put the bedding in with the bodies. She did the same with the bedroom as she did the bathroom.

"Did you hire a cleaning crew?" La asked she knew she did not have to clean up after herself nor did she need a cleaning crew but you could never be too careful.

"Always on staff!" Jah reassured her.

"Who's next?" La La asked.

Dear Readers,

I hope you enjoyed these two stories, because this is just the beginning of the women of XXX The Underground Playgrounds. There are four women left to give you their revengeful twisted stories . Please take the time to leave an helpful review for other readers. Thank you and I appreciate your support.

Salute
Ms. Pantha Jones

www.ingramcontent.com/pod-product-compliance
Lightning Source LLC
Chambersburg PA
CBHW070923180626
46817CB00003B/1177